SYLOR

CONQUERED WORLD: BOOK NINE

ELIN WYN

CLOCK
WALK
PUBLISHING

NESTA

It has never been a good idea to scream in the tunnels.

The darkness had its secret inhabitants and sometimes shadows were more than what they seemed. The mere sound of footsteps was enough to draw unwanted attention in the cramped tunnels below Nyheim, and caution was the number one tool to carry if you wanted to survive in the underground. And if you ventured deep into the tunnels, you needed more than just caution.

You needed silence.

"SON OF A BITCH!" I cried out as loud as I could, looking down as blood trickled out my cracked fingernail.

Yes, just a fingernail.

But it was the last straw.

My voice echoed through the maze of tunnels behind me, but I didn't care if someone (or something) could hear me. My broken nail demanded all my attention, and I would scream as loudly as possible if that helped ease the pain.

Caution and silence?

Screw that.

Sitting down on a pile of rubble, flashlight strapped to my shoulder, I brought my finger up to my mouth and sucked on the blood as I grimaced. The coppery taste of my own blood made my stomach growl in protest, and I remembered once more just how hungry I really was.

For a moment, I wondered if any Xathi had survived the war. Maybe some of them had snuck underground, feeding on helpless prey while growing fat. I wouldn't mind having one of the bastards find me right now. I'd carve them up really good, light a fire, and make a career as a Xathi chef. I was pretty sure the spidery assholes would taste like crap, but as long as they weren't poisonous, I wouldn't complain. Light a fire, sprinkle some herbs on there, maybe some pepper, as well...

"Focus," I said to myself out loud, my voice bouncing off the cramped walls of the tunnel. Imagination would do nothing to keep my belly full.

Sighing audibly, I ran one hand through my hair, pushing it all back, and eyed the pile of rubble in front of me. Stones with jagged edges were blocking the entrance to a smaller tunnel, one I knew as well as the lines on the palm of my hand. That little burrow had been carved by me, after all, and it had been the place I had started calling home after the first Xathi incursions.

It wasn't the best place to live if you hated tight places. In fact, I didn't want to be here now.

But I needed food. And so I'd returned to find my old abode.

It wasn't cozy—it was nothing but a hole in the stone, one sheltered from view by the blankets I had hung by the entrance—but that was the place where I had stashed my dingy possessions. Not that I cared about possessions, truth be told. The only thing I cared about in that moment was the pack of dried meat I was certain was among my things.

And so, I got to work.

Down on my knees, I started pushing the rubble out of the way with both hands. Beads of sweat started appearing on my forehead, and my stomach growled louder and louder with each movement. After half an hour or so, though, the rubble finally gave way, creating a small entrance that allowed me to squeeze myself into my little burrow.

"You've gotta be shitting me," I said, ignoring the small pile of dirty clothing on the corner and focusing on the packet of dried meat. It sat abandoned in one of the burrow's corners, the package torn open by the edge of a stone that had fallen from the ceiling. Inside it, fat and happy insects were busy banqueting on whatever was left of the meat.

Gritting my teeth, I kicked the packet as hard as I could, hissing in frustration. I couldn't believe I had wasted so much time digging through the rubble just to find out worms had stolen my lunch. But what was a woman to do? In a world where spaceships brimming with spidery assholes fell from the sky, and even the plants themselves were doing their best to get rid of you, there was no other option but to be tough.

Squeezing myself out of the burrow, I collected my backpack from the floor and slung it over my shoulder. No use in crying over spilt milk...or lunch-eating worms, for that matter. Besides, I had survived worse. No parents, raised by a criminal, and then establishing myself as a high-ranking member of an underground gang: a true survivor's curriculum.

Life had never been easy, but if I were to be honest, I'd had it good for a while.

Being a skilled contrabandist had its perks, and the underground was the perfect place for someone like me to thrive. Then, of course, came the Xathi...and after that, those stupid giant vines. Lifechanging events for the entire population, and even more so for those who dwelled underground.

The Xathi attacks had made sure food shortages started being a daily occurrence, and when the vine dome took over the city, it all got worse. My little burrow got destroyed by the vines moving underground and even Odeon, my mentor and leader of our gang, vanished. Sabre, our gang of rogues and misfits, pretty much disbanded without Odeon's leadership.

And without a leader and food, Sabre was nothing more than a pretty name.

But maybe getting the gang back together was exactly what I needed to do. Our members were competent, and I was pretty sure that, with some strategizing and team effort, we could rebuild whatever was left of the underground.

It was with that thought in mind that I made my way through the tunnels, this time being more careful about it. The underground was a pretty safe place, all things considered, as long as you remained in the main caverns complex and the adjacent tunnels. If you ventured deeper, though, nobody could really guarantee your safety. As for me, I didn't mind trading safety for a little privacy.

"Nesta, where have you been?" An old man croaked,

standing up as I reached the end of the tunnel. I could only see his silhouette, his figure outlined by the warm lights flooding the cavern behind me. "Have you been looking for food? I don't have anything to trade, but I—"

"No food, Samuel," I said as I walked past him, ignoring his outstretched hand. "Not today." I heard him curse something, but I paid it no heed. My mind was already at work as I tried to think of a way to bring the gang together.

The first step?

A visit to Buke's, a large tent at the end of the cavern that doubled as a bar and canteen. Of course, now that there was no food to go around, the place was nothing but a gathering place for the underground's hard-hitting drinkers. Whoever of the old crew had remained underground, they had to be there.

I made my way through a sea of tents and merchants' carts, ignoring everyone's pleas for food. They all knew me as Nesta, the right hand of the Sabre's leader, and they were probably thinking I had a stash of food hidden someplace deep in the tunnels. Yeah, as if.

"Alright, Nesta," I muttered under my breath, standing before Buke's entrance. "Time to show these assholes what you're made of." With a deep breath, I ducked under the entrance, nothing but a large canvas supported by two tall logs, and silence immediately took over the room.

"Hey, assholes," I grinned, hands in my pockets as I stared at the four guys huddled at a low table in the corner. They were sitting on dusty old pillows, their legs folded, and tall pitchers of diluted beer sat in front of them. Life wasn't going well for them, that much I could tell. Any other time, and I would've found them here laughing raucously, their cheeks already tinged a drunkard's red. As it was, their faces had been hollowed out by hunger, and their expressions were grim. "You look like shit, the lot of you."

"You're one to talk," Stupid Joe threw back at me, slowly getting up to his feet. A tall bald-headed man, he looked imposing right up to the point where you found even a kid could trick him. He was probably the most gullible person I had ever met, but he compensated by having the quickest fingers in the whole of the underground. He could snatch a purse from someone's pocket and nobody would notice. "Where the hell have you been, Nesta?"

"Me?" I said with a smirk. "I found a goldmine, and set myself up as the Queen of the Underground. I came here to invite you to my palace."

"Really?" Stupid Joe's eyes lit up. "Will there be food in your palace?"

"C'mon, man," one of the other men, Topan, sighed. "She's just messing with you."

"Oh," he said, lowering his head as he sunk back onto his pillow. He grabbed his beer with a sad expression, and his belly rumbled with a desperate tone.

"What do you want, Nesta?" Topan continued, this time turning his attention to me. He was slightly shorter than the other men, but he had the kind of attitude that made others follow him. "Did you come to share the food you have hidden? Because if not, you can turn around and crawl back to whatever hole you just came from."

"Is that your way of saying you miss me?" I said, deadpan. "You're not as stupid as those assholes out there, are you? You know damn well that I don't have any food hidden. If I had, you guys would have been the first to know."

"Would we?" he queried. "Because I remember Odeon and you keeping secrets from the rest of us all the time. Who's to say the two of you didn't stockpile food behind our backs?"

"Odeon's dead, asshole," I sighed.

"I know that," he shrugged. "Is that why you're here? Do you want to be the Sabre's newest leader?"

"I don't—"

"You were Odeon's little pet, sure, but that doesn't

mean shit anymore. Sabre has disbanded." Locking his eyes on mine, he gritted his teeth. "And, for the record, Odeon was an asshole."

"He did what he needed to do," I tried, even though I already knew my words were useless. These guys' minds were already made up. "The underground thrived under him."

"Really?" Topan said. "The way I see it, he just used Sabre to lead a comfortable life. Now, don't get me wrong...I want a comfortable life as much as the next guy. I just don't think the way Odeon did it was the right one. We should have been making money off the assholes on the surface," he continued, pointing with his thumb toward the ceiling, "not surviving on the back of those on the underground."

"You're wrong about Odeon," I hissed.

"Am I?"

"Yeah, you are, you dipshit." Shaking my head, I closed my eyes for a second to gather my thoughts and then turned on my heels. "Fine, if you want to stay hidden in here, go right ahead. Good luck trying to survive on that piss you call beer."

Without giving them the time for a reply, I marched out of Buke's. For a moment, I simply stood there, taking in the sad scene in front of me. While before the Xathi the underground thrived, now it looked more and more like a refugee camp with each passing day. I had no idea how the few hundred people that lived in here would survive, but I wasn't about to curl up on the floor and wait for my turn to die.

I was a survivor...and so I would survive.

Even if I had to do it on the surface.

SYLOR

I t had been nine days, and slightly more than eleven
hours, since the city was entombed by the vines of
the 'Puppet Master.' It had been eight days, and just
under four hours, since General Rouhr tasked Strike
Team Two with discovering a way through the vines
and back into the 'outside' world.

We had made numerous attempts, seventeen to be
exact, and thus far, nothing had worked. The
frustration upon all of our minds was palpable and a
nuisance. The very idea that a mere vegetable had been
able to thwart our every attempt, our patently superior
technology, was confounding and absurd.

Nothing that we had tried had amounted to
anything more than a measly scratch, a scratch that was
healed in less than an hour. Whatever this creature was,

it was not something that followed the laws and sense of reality. It was my job, by the order of General Rouhr, to do what was necessary in order to find a way through the vines, and I was not about to let seventeen failures deter me.

The typical Valorni warrior was slap-dash and crude. He used his fists if he didn't have a blaster. He used a blaster and blasted his enemy with wild abandon and bloodlust.

That was not me.

I hated the stereotypical Valorni behavior.

I tried to be as precise as possible. It wasn't always easy. My speech differed from Axtin, but contact with humans kept me in practice of using some vernacular.

It had become apparent that standard weapons and attacks would not be enough. Even attacks that by all sense and reason should have worked, had failed. So, it was now time to begin the progression from conventional to the unconventional.

It was time for me to speak with the botanist and the chemist. I needed to work with Tella and Leena.

After I arrived at their joint laboratory on the other side of General Rouhr's building, I implored them to use their abilities and knowledge for any sort of assistance they could give. As I walked into the office they shared, I smiled as genuinely as I could. "Good afternoon, ladies."

Leena looked up from a small microscope and returned my smile. Hers was genuine and real, even though it had not been in her nature to be kind and affable. "Afternoon, Sylor. Was there anything you needed?"

"They always need something," Tella snapped from her corner. "They don't come to see us otherwise." I knew that she was attempting to make a joke, to be funny, but there seemed to be a bit of an underlying resentment to her words. Perhaps it was that Tella was not the sort to enjoy confinement, and the vines of this creature were doing exactly that.

"Tella," Leena admonished. Apparently, her statement truly had been an attempt at humor. Leena turned back to me and motioned me to come in. As I did, she left her station and approached me. "So, what can we do for you, Sylor?"

There was a small sense of gratification to hear her say my name. Many of the humans still only knew me as one of 'those aliens.'

I did not blame them for their reactions to me, I was one of the foreigners that had brought war and destruction to their home.

But still, acknowledgement of my person was appreciated.

"Dr. Dewitt," I responded. "I have been tasked with finding a way, conventional or not, through the vines.

We have made seventeen separate attempts and have failed seventeen times. I come to you seeking advice and a new set of minds to think of ideas."

"Well, now aren't you all proper and civilized," Tella commented, a half-smile twisting her lips. She waved a hand. "I don't mean anything by it, I'm just not used to it. Takar tries to be all high-and-mighty when he talks to me, but he's almost as crazy as his brother. It's a bit odd, hearing it from a Valorni."

"Tella!" Leena said with a sharp look. "That's rude!"

I held up my hand to put an end to Leena's reprimand. "It's alright. She is entitled to her opinion." I looked over at Tella. "To answer your question, my mannerisms are my own. There is nothing more to it, nor do I intend any, as you put it 'high-and-mightiness'. Now, is that enough of an answer for you?"

Tella shrugged, nodded, then returned to what she had been working on when I entered. I turned my attention back to Leena. "Would you be able to assist me?"

Leena stood still for a few breaths before finally answering. "I don't know." She reached out and placed her hand on my arm as I started to turn away. "I didn't say that we won't. What I meant was that I'm not sure if we'll be able to help. If everything that you've done has failed, I'm not sure what we can do."

"With your expertise in chemicals," I nodded at

Leena, "and your expertise in plant life," I added with a nod to Tella, "I hope to gain some additional suggestions as to what we may be able to do."

Tella gave a sort of half shrug and arched an eyebrow as she sat in her chair. "The only thing that I can think of that had any sort of effect was the toxin." She looked at Leena, a look of disappointment adorning her face. "But we don't have enough to use."

My hopes had been dashed before they had been given a glimmer of life. Leena sighed and walked to a small row of cabinets on a near wall. She unlocked a glass door and retrieved a small vial. "This is all that we have. It's not enough for what you need, and not enough for us to synthesize."

"Besides," Tella cut in, "I'm not sure we want to find more anyway."

"Why is that?" I asked.

She rose from her chair and looked out the only window in the lab. "Take a look out there," she instructed me. I stepped over to the window. Her finger pointed to the vines. "Those things came up, out of the ground, and barely caused any damage. I know that a few buildings were destroyed, and a few people died, but Puppet Master went out of its way to make sure that we were closed in, not hurt. What if that changes with the toxin?"

"And what if it does?" I asked.

She rolled her eyes and huffed. "I really wish you overgrown brutes would learn to think things through." She pointed to one of the massive pillar-like vines a few blocks over. "Think about what damage that one vine there could cause if it fell. Are you willing to risk that?"

"So, you're afraid of some collateral damage? Is that what you're saying?" I asked.

"Of course, that's what I'm saying," she practically shrieked. "What if some of that 'collateral damage' is a life? What if some of that damage is the death of a child, or one of your own? What then?"

Before I had the opportunity to answer, Leena added her own opinion and fear to the argument. "Tella's right. If the toxin works on the vines the way it worked on some of the other plants, the damage potential would be catastrophic."

"I understand that, but if it wasn't," I countered. "What if we used the toxin upon a small section of the vines, caused it pain, and the vines retreated? We must not allow ourselves to be locked away in a dome like prisoners with no attempt to fight back. This creature must be shown that we will not go lightly."

"You're an idiot," Tella huffed. "I want out."

"I apologize," I said. "I don't understand what you mean."

"What I mean," Tella said, punctuating each word with a tilt of the head, "is that I'm done with this. I will not participate in this. The potential harm to the city and her people is too big, too much. I won't be part of it." With that, she turned away from us and left, Leena trying to call her back.

Leena turned back to me. "She has a point. The damage that could result is..."

"I understand," I interrupted. "However, to surrender to an enemy, that is something that cannot be permitted. We cannot simply give in to this...this... creature and expect it to simply leave us alone. It is routinely invading everyone's homes with its tendrils. It has forced us to use auxiliary power sources, and we will soon be out of resources. What are we supposed to do then?"

"I don't know," Leena admitted.

"I ask for your help because you are one of the smartest people I have ever had the privilege of meeting, and we need to find a method of escape." I looked at Leena in earnest. "General Rouhr has tasked me with finding a way through the vines, and I require your intellect to find a way. What do you say? Can we make a more powerful version of the chemical grenade you created?"

She was hesitant, and I could see that she was unwilling to assist, but her sense of duty and understanding won through. She eventually nodded.

We began our work, and after many hours of toil,

we finally had a chemical bomb that was, if our calculations were correct, the most powerful that either of us had ever come across.

"Thank you. I mean it," I said quietly as I gently, ever so gently, laid it into a case that we had created for its transport.

Leena merely nodded, the look on her face telling me everything I needed to know about her feelings. I placed a hand on her shoulder, thanked her for her assistance, and left, carrying the case with the bomb with me. I walked slowly and carefully towards our testing ground, hoping that this would be enough to accomplish the task at hand.

NESTA

I hated the surface.

It was noisy everywhere I went, so much I could barely hear my own thoughts. The whole city seemed to be submerged in a chorus of loud voices, and the growl of shuttle engines as they zoomed back and forth overhead didn't seem to help. Never mind the giant green dome of vines that encased the whole place. Just looking up at its domed surface made me feel as if I were a tiny fish in some creepy alien aquarium.

I kept the hood of my ragged cloak up, doing my best to blend in with the crowd, but I quickly realized I didn't need any of that. The crowded streets and back alleys were brimming with people, and everyone seemed too preoccupied about their daily lives to give a damn about some bony woman wearing a dirty old cloak.

"Sol Avenue," I read from a sign, doing my best to recall the city layout. If I followed the avenue, I should be able to find the farmer's market...which meant I should be able to find some food.

I was pretty sure that the vines had cut off the city from the rest of the planet, and that the city must've been running low on food, but I tried to keep my hopes up. As bad as the situation probably was, I didn't see anyone assaulting whoever committed the sin of carrying a bag of vegetables down the street. I took that as a good omen, silencing my inner critic as it tried to convince me that the surface idiots were just too civilized to do something as lowly as steal food.

At the end of the avenue, my heart started jumping happily as I saw dozens of street stalls lining the walls of buildings. Merchants called after the potential customers with loud voices, but few people stopped. Some of them glanced warily at the food carts that seemed to pop up every hundred feet or so, but almost everyone kept their heads low and carried on. Either people weren't going hungry, or they had no money to spend on food.

Well, I was definitely hungry, and the fact that I had no money was just a detail.

"Greetings, good sir," I said with the largest smile I

could conjure, approaching one of the vendors. I had no idea how polite I should act when dealing with surface street vendors, but I quickly decided that being as pompous as I could was a great idea.

"Hey," he said, an annoyed expression on his face. He eyed me curiously and, pursing his lips, folded his arms over his chest. Then, with a quick gesture, he threw some old blanket over the fruit in his stall. "No money, no food."

"What? Who the hell said I didn't have any money?" I found myself saying, already clenching my fists.

"Have you looked in a mirror recently?" he continued, his serious expression giving way to a mocking grin. I noticed he was missing teeth as his lips curled up and, for a moment, I imagined how it'd feel to make him lose another tooth or two. "Where the hell have you crawled out from? A mine?"

"Who the hell—"

"Do I think I am?" he finished for me. "The guy who won't sell you any food...unless you can pay for it, that is."

"Of course I can pay," I lied. Credits really dropped in value after everything went to shit, at least when it came to the underworld, and I hadn't bothered with carrying any these past few weeks. Not a problem: I'd pay this asshole with my fists. "Show me the goods."

"The goods?" he snorted. "What are you? Some hardened criminal?"

Briefly, I wondered if his teeth would have any value in the underground market. Maybe I wasn't meant to be a Xathi chef, after all. Perhaps it was my destiny to become a vendor of handmade collars made out of assholes' teeth. Not my first choice but, hey, you don't get to choose the talents you're born with.

Shaking his head, the man finally reached for the blanket covering his fruit and pulled it back. I looked down, my fingers already twitching as I imagined myself with a big fat apple in my hands, but what I found wasn't what I was expecting.

"What the hell's that?" I asked, frowning as I realized he wasn't selling fruit, after all. There were round pieces of bread on a tray, but they seemed almost as old as I was, blots of a sickly green mold covering their cracked surfaces.

"Food," he responded, quickly throwing his blanket over the tray again. "Now, pay up or get out of my way."

"I'll spend my money somewhere else, asshole," I finally said, holding my chin up before turning my back to him. My stomach grumbled in protest, the moldy bread looking more appetizing with each passing second, but I held strong. If I was going to steal something, I definitely wouldn't settle for something that seemed more mold than bread.

Stalking away from the mold vendor, I ambled down the avenue while paying close attention to whatever the vendors were trying to sell. Almost all fruit looked as if it were slowly rotting, all bread seemed to have mold in it, and there was barely any meat to be seen. It seemed that life wasn't being kind for anyone.

"Excuse me, miss," I heard a tired voice say from right behind me, and I quickly turned around to find an old woman standing there. She was pushing a cart loaded with apples down the avenue, and even though the apples didn't look freshly picked, they sure as hell seemed edible. In fact, the more I looked at them, the more they started looking like the best damn thing on the entire planet.

Taking one step back, I jumped out of the woman's way and she slowly went back to pushing her cart, groaning with the effort. She looked frail and tired, her face covered with wrinkles. Someone's grandmother, of that I had no doubt. "Let me help you with that," I said, standing next to her and laying both my hands on the cart. "Where to?"

"Oh, bless you," she smiled, pointing with her finger straight ahead. "Just at the end of the street. I'm taking these to my son's stall. I would do it myself, but my bones...getting old, you see."

"I see," I said as I smiled back at her, happily letting her lead the way.

I couldn't help but notice how some people greedily stared at the apples in the cart, but none of them seemed as if they were about to try something. You'd think that a war against spider-psychopaths from outer space would have given the surface folk an edge, but they seemed pretty civilized. I wondered if that had something to do with the aliens that had settled in the city. The bastards looked tough enough, so if they had taken it upon themselves to maintain the order...

"Here we are," the old woman said, pointing to a stall right beside her. In it, a portly man in his fifties was busy haggling with a woman carrying two small kids. "I know it's not much, but..." Still smiling, the woman reached for her cart and grabbed one of the apples. She threw it in my direction and I caught it midair, my stomach immediately coming alive as I felt the smooth surface of the apple under my fingertips.

"Thank you!" I exclaimed, already burying my teeth into it, juice dripping down my chin. It tasted amazing, perhaps the best meal of my entire life. Apparently, going for days without food was a good method of improving one's palate.

Hunger *really* is the best sauce.

Busy with wolfing down the apple, I only noticed the old woman had disappeared when I was about to thank her once more. She had joined whatever argument her son was having on the other corner of the stall, and she had left her apple cart unattended. I was about to call to her when another idea crawled into my mind.

Holding the half-apple I still had between my teeth, I closed in on the cart and went for the apples. Being as discrete as I could, I started stuffing them inside my ratty blouse, hoping that the way I had my cloak wrapped around my body would be enough to hide my spoils.

"Sorry," I quietly mouthed, throwing one last look at the old woman before I turned around. I started going down the avenue hurriedly.

Guilt ruined any excitement I should have felt at the score.

Food was scarce.

Fresh fruit was a hot commodity in the underground marketplace, and I knew I'd make some good trades with the dozen apples I was carrying inside my blouse.

Worse-case scenario, I'd just eat them all.

Maybe the surface wasn't that bad, after all.

Maybe I should visit more often.

I made a sharp turn at the end of the street when I felt something tug on the back of my cloak. "What the...?" I muttered, a massive green hand grabbing me by the bicep. I was spun around fast, only to come face to face with a man way taller than I was. Except, of course, he wasn't a man.

At least, not a human.

There was intelligence in the way his eyes glinted, but his body looked far more powerful than anything I had seen before. Even though he was wearing what looked like tactical gear, I could almost *feel* the way his hard muscles rippled under the surface of his green skin. If he wanted, I had no doubt he could pick me up and break me over his knee like a twig.

I had to be careful around this one.

"You stole from that woman," the green alien said. "You're going to jail."

And, just like that, being careful was out of fashion.

Gritting my teeth, I laid one hand on his wrist and, applying some pressure on the articulation, peeled his fingers off my shoulder. Then I gained as much balance as I could and sent my right foot flying against one of his ankles. The impact was brutal.

On me.

"Shit," I groaned, falling to the ground as pain travelled up my leg from my toes. "What are you made of? Stone?"

"I saw you steal from that woman," he declared, completely ignoring my totally relevant question. "Return those apples right now."

"What apples?" I asked, putting on what I hoped to be a look of pure innocence. It didn't help that, in that moment, the apples I had tucked inside my blouse rolled out from under me, one of them stopping right before the green alien's feet.

Shaking his head, he sighed audibly. "You're coming with me," he said, grabbing me by the scruff of my neck to pull me to my feet. As he did it, I noticed that he wasn't alone. There was a blonde woman with him, and she was already busy with picking my apples from the ground.

Defeated, I watched as she went back to the old woman's stall to return them. When she came back, I presented her with my best frown. She just ignored me, strutting down the avenue with the boundless energy that came with a full stomach.

"What now?" I asked my green captor as he pushed me down street, trailing after the blonde woman.

"Now you shut up," was all he said.

It was official: the surface sucked.

SYLOR

The delay that this young woman had caused was an annoyance. While it was true that we did not have an official deadline, it was necessary that we discover a way through the vines quickly enough in order to get supplies and resources. Having to stop for this…woman…who had been stealing from a little old woman, that was an inconvenience that had only slowed us down.

I couldn't quite tell how old she was, but she looked to be far too young to have to resort to thievery in order to survive. And as for why she was stealing here, when we had put in the effort to ensure that everyone was properly cared for to the best of our collective abilities, that confused me.

As we continued to make our way to the testing site,

I noticed that Leena made no move to hide her curiosity of the woman. She was looking her up and down and studying her as though she were some sort of new species.

I wasn't sure what it was that she was trying to discover about her, but the woman looked uncomfortable with Leena's stares. Not that I cared, she was a thief. Thieves had no rights in my eyes. If she was uncomfortable being around Leena and me, that was just too bad. As we walked, I took a closer look at our thief. She was dirty, clad in terribly fitting clothing, and looked to be a bit underweight.

Wherever this woman had been living, it wasn't conducive to a healthy life. Seeing how thin she was, not a healthy thin like Mira or Mariella, but a "I-haven't-eaten-properly-in-months" kind, almost made me feel more empathetic towards her. If she could somehow manage to get some weight on her, there would be a possibility of her no longer needing to steal.

Her dark-colored hair was dirty, matted in a few places, and barely fell to the nape of her neck. I could see that she must have had it cut often, but whoever cut her hair for her was terrible at it. Her hair was uneven and looked fuller in some places and thinner in others. Her skin, a shade or two darker than Leena's, was dirty, as if she hadn't seen a bath or shower in weeks. If she had been clean, and possibly with a little more weight on her so she didn't look so skeletal, she may have been an attractive young lady.

She glared at me as I studied her. "Well?" she said with definite attitude in her voice.

"Well, what?" I asked her as we turned down a street that used to have a name, but I had never learned it.

"Have you gotten your fill staring at me? Or did you want me to strip naked so you can see everything?" She didn't bother holding back her scorn and I found myself hardly blaming her. "The way the two of you are working me over with your eyes, I feel like I should just strip right now so you can get the full picture."

"That will not be necessary," I commented. "However, your indignation is unwarranted at the moment. If you had not been stealing from that old woman, you would not be in this situation. Your current predicament is entirely of your own doing."

She shook her head in what I assumed to be bewilderment. "I'm sorry...what? 'Indignation'? 'Predicament'? What the hell are you saying to me?"

"He's saying," Leena answered, "that if you weren't a little thief, you wouldn't be in trouble right now. Is that easier to understand?"

"Why didn't he just say so from the beginning?"

Leena let out a bark of laughter that made the woman sidestep. "He did. I think you need to work on your vocabulary a little bit. What's your name?"

"Why should I tell you?" she shot back.

"The reason for answering the question is to prevent us from referring to you simply as 'thief'." I answered. "Or do you like being called something based on your profession?"

She glared at me and visibly thought about what I said. With a roll of her eyes and a long sigh, she finally conceded. "My name is Nesta."

I was unsure as to the truth of her answer, but my limited knowledge of human naming rights prevented me from disputing her.

"Very well, Nesta. My name is Sylor, and she is Leena," I introduced.

"Why are you telling me your names?" Nesta asked. "You're supposedly my captors, so why would you give me your names?"

It was my turn to shrug as I shifted the case with the chemical bomb to my other arm. "What would you be able to do with our names?"

This visibly confused her as she opened her mouth several times to answer but did not. "Fine. Where are you taking me? This doesn't look like a place where jails would be." She was twisting and turning around, looking at the area in which we were. It was a residential portion of the city, one of the ones that had been abandoned during the Xathi attack and never reoccupied. The homes looked torn apart from the inside out. She yelped as a set of tendrils came down from above and began searching several homes.

With a smile, I shook my head at her surprise. We followed the street through the residential area to a small clearing that had once been a park. The members of Strike Team Two were there, trying again to pierce the vine-wall using tactics that had already been found to be useless.

Rokul was trying to burn the vines using a modified flamethrower that was able to produce white fire, a much hotter flame than conventional flamethrowers were able to provide. After a few moments of him attempting to burn the vines, he stepped away and Takar went in with his oversized saw and tried to cut into the vines.

As we approached, I could see that the tactic had merit, but it proved to be fruitless. Rokul's curses filled the air as he punched the vine.

"I see that you've improved upon your vocabulary," I quipped as we approached.

"Shut up, Sylor," he shot back. "Who's your new friend? She's a little dirty."

Before I could answer, Nesta shot back at Rokul. "Oh, yeah, make fun of the poor homeless woman. At least I'm not an inconsiderate ass that looks like a damn fruit. And who cut your hair, that idiot with the saw?

Oh, I see you guys have the same hair cut…must have gotten a discount at 'idiot-haircuts-r-us,' huh?"

With wide eyes, Rokul looked between Nesta and me. "Well, you managed to find yourself a fun little friend, Sylor." His face broke out into a massive smile as she spoke. "I like her. So, what does she do?"

"She's a thief. We caught her stealing from a member of the elder class," I answered.

"Then why bring her here?" Karzin asked.

I turned to my commander and handed over the case. "Careful, that's our newest chemical bomb. It's volatile." He took the case carefully and set it down slowly. "As to your inquiry, commander, I felt it prudent to bring that," I pointed at the case, "rather than waste time escorting Nesta to prison. I will take her when we have completed our tests."

He gave me a look, then looked beyond me to Leena. "Leena."

"Karzin," she responded. I noticed that she stayed behind Nesta, and that Iq'her had joined her shortly after I said the word 'thief.'

"What's going on here?" Nesta asked, but I did not feel inclined to respond.

"Tell me what's in the case," Karzin ordered. I went on to explain that Leena and I had worked diligently on creating a bigger, more potent, and more volatile chemical bomb. The specifics of the bomb were a source of pride for me and I was glad that Karzin tolerated my need to explain the technical side of things.

Technology was something of a passion for me. I often competed and worked with Sakev on adapting our weapons, both personal and for the ship...when it existed...as well as modifying the technology that we used in order to do whatever we needed. Case in point, after losing two fingers from my left hand, I had created a special sleeve that encompassed my left arm. The sleeve was outfitted with a miniature computer system with a touchscreen, a back-up comm unit, and a small scanner that would allow me to scan any unknown substances.

"So," he interrupted me. "Will it work?"

"I sincerely hope so, sir," I answered. "If it does not, then I no longer have an idea of what to do."

"Then let's do it," Karzin said. We placed the chemical bomb at the base of the vines, set the timer, and backed away behind a nearby home.

"I suggest putting on a mask," I said to the others. I quickly took a mask, tossed it to Leena, tossed another to Nesta, and put one on myself. The bomb went off with a massive explosion, sending debris and dirt everywhere. When the smoke finally cleared enough for me to move forward, I activated the fan unit in the carrying case and sucked away all the gas and smoke.

When it was cleared, all there was to be seen was a gash in the ground, and vines that seemed to be untouched.

I chanced a look back at the rest of the team and observed the disappointment, shock, and bewilderment upon their faces. Leena looked to be as frustrated as I felt, while Karzin looked defeated.

"I don't think your little plan worked," Nesta's muffled voice floated in the air. Her words carried with them a sense of ridicule and loss. "Just what was your plan, exactly?"

I ignored her and looked to Leena. She held her arms out and shook her head. She had no answers, and neither did I. I looked back to the explosion site and stared at the hole in the ground, a terrible reminder of our failure.

NESTA

"Were you trying to massage those vines?" I insisted, crossing my legs as I sat on the ground. "Or maybe you were trying to tickle them?" I scratched my chin as I said it, trying to look as innocent as possible, even though I knew I was getting on Sylor's nerves. He gave me a frown, then turned his attention back to the wisps of smoke still rising from the ground, near the unscathed vines. One of his team members snorted, but quickly hid his amused expression when Sylor glared at him.

"We're trying to destroy those vines," the blonde woman, Leena, said. She was standing right next to me, looking at the green wall of vines with a pensive expression. "This here...it was a prototype bomb we hoped would help us."

"Didn't work that well, did it?" I asked, looking straight ahead at the vines.

The blast had seemed like a serious one, intense enough to blow up a brick wall, but the vines looked completely unharmed. I had no idea what they really were, but if these serious-looking aliens and their bombs couldn't blow a hole through the barrier, then Nyheim was in serious trouble. My little stroll through the market was enough for me to know that food was quickly becoming a scarce resource, and without food, it wouldn't take long before the whole city descended into chaos.

"No, Nesta," Leena sighed, not even bothering trying to hide her concern, "it didn't work at all."

"Are you in charge of these guys?" I asked her, trying to sound polite. She didn't look as if she were afraid of them. In fact, she looked completely at ease. Maybe if I got on her good side, I'd manage to convince her to let me go.

"No, not really," she replied, finally looking away from the vines and turning her gaze to me. "I'm just a chemist. I'm doing my best to help them find a solution to this, uhm, situation...but it hasn't been exactly easy."

"Nothing's easy nowadays," I said casually, trying to ignore the hole in my stomach. The apple I had eaten had felt like a feast, but now that I had nothing else to eat, I seemed to have become even hungrier than before. As if to agree with me, my stomach rumbled audibly.

"What about you, Nesta?" Leena asked me, curiosity dancing in her eyes. She eyed my dirty clothes for a while, and then offered me a kind smile. I couldn't stop myself from frowning. I didn't enjoy when strangers were kind to me. Kindness was just one heartbeat away from turning into pity, and if there was something I *really* despised, it was being pitied.

"I'm just a nobody," I shrugged, slowly pushing myself up to my feet. I let my eyes scan my surroundings, hoping that I'd find a way out of this mess, but Sylor had his vigilant gaze on me. If I tried to make a run for it, the bastard would just squash me under his gigantic hands.

"A nobody who isn't above stealing from an old woman," Leena continued. I had a scathing remark ready for her, but I stopped myself when I noticed she wasn't saying it out of malice. Usually, I didn't react that well to kindness, but in her case...

"Look, I was just hungry, alright?" I sighed. "I'm not exactly proud I had to steal from that lady, but what was I supposed to do? I have nothing else. The vines even took my damn home."

"Where was it, your home? Lua District?"

"Yeah," I lied. "I mean, not exactly...but close."

"It'll be fine," Leena smiled, laying one hand on my

shoulder. I flinched under her touch but, thankfully, she didn't even notice it. "Once we figure a way out of this dome, everything will go back to normal."

"Don't get too friendly with the thief, Leena," Sylor said, his back to us as he packed up his gear. Some of his teammates were busy with collecting samples from the place where they had detonated the bomb, but most of them were just milling around with bored expressions on their faces. It seemed they weren't that hopeful about a breakthrough when it came to the vine situation.

"Did any of those vines crawl up your ass?" I couldn't stop myself from asking him. "You're looking a little green there, buddy."

"My skin pigmentation is typical to one of the Valorni race," he replied and, for a moment, I didn't know what to say. I didn't even know if he was mocking me or if he was being serious. Closing the distance between the two of us, he stopped a mere two feet away from me. "As for you...is 'dirty' your natural skin color?"

"Asshole," I growled, cocking my arm back, only to send my fist flying toward his chest. I hit it right in the center, between his pectorals, and pain shot up my arm. Apparently, trying to kick or punch a muscular alien, who was part of a violent race, all while he's wearing tactical gear, remained a stupid idea.

"Your derogatory terms are amusing," he snorted and, before I could do anything about it, he rested both hands on my hips and lifted me up. He threw me over his shoulder and, after barking a few orders to the other aliens, turned around and started walking back the way we'd come, Leena trailing after us.

"Is he always like this?" I asked Leena, trying to forget how embarrassed I was to be carried through the streets like a sack of potatoes.

"Pretty much," she said, smiling. As for me, the best I could manage was another frown. Being carried to jail by a green alien wasn't exactly putting me in a good mood. I spent the rest of the way brooding, occasionally punching Sylor between his shoulder blades, to no effect.

When we finally arrived at our destination, a nondescript building right in the center of the city, we were saluted by two human soldiers guarding the gate. Sylor grunted his acknowledgement and we went inside, my eyes peeled back as I tried to memorize every turn he took.

If I wanted to get out of this place, I had to pay attention.

"What's that?" a Valorni soldier laughed as we finally arrived at the detention center, a long, cramped room with holding cells on either side. Instead of bars, the cells seemed to have heavy-duty doors, the kind one wouldn't get past without brute force, considerable time, or lockpicks. "You know damn well humans aren't that tasty, Sylor. And that one looks bony as a Skotan bat."

"Don't scare her," Sylor said, as serious as ever. Ignoring the other Valorni's laugh, he simply strolled inside one of the cells and put me down on top of the bed. I stood up immediately, but he stepped out fast, pressing his open hand against a panel, and ordered the door to close. It swung fast on its hinges, despite how heavy it seemed. "Don't cause any trouble," he warned me, looking straight into my eyes. "You're going to be here for a while."

"How long?"

"The punishment for stealing something minor is usually one month in the holding cells," he said. One month wasn't that bad, I thought. Sure, I would be stuck inside this crappy room for the duration, but at least I would be fed... or so I hoped. "But, considering that Nyheim is in a state of emergency, the normal sentences don't apply. Punishment for the dishonest handling of resources has gone up to nine months."

"NINE MONTHS?" I shouted, barely believing what I was hearing. How the hell was I supposed to remain stuck in this place for nine freaking months? I'd go insane before my time was up.

"Nine months," Sylor repeated. Then he merely

turned on his heels and started walking out. He hesitated for a moment, and looked back at me over his shoulder. "Goodbye, thief."

Feeling dejected, I watched him walk out, then sat back down on the bed. Nine months of jail time? If Sylor thought I'd accept that like a good little woman, then he was in for a surprise. No way in hell was I going to accept that.

I had to find a way out...and fast.

SYLOR

There were too many variables that I still did not know in terms of what was needed to find our way through the vines. I had done what was obvious, done what was simple, and done what made sense. None of it was successful.

I had moved on to unconventional, over-the-top, and potentially insane. None of those had worked, either. Eighteen different tactics chosen, eighteen different methods used—all of which led to one ending...failure. Pure, simple, inescapable failure.

And several complaints about Nesta.

How the guards were incapable of dealing with one woman, one solitary, underweight woman, escaped me. However, I've already had four complaints about her, and it had yet to reach lunch time.

I contemplated making a complaint of my own regarding the guards, but I knew that it would do nothing. Instead, my concentration was centered on how and why my attempts had failed. I had never had a weapon design fail. They had always done what they were designed to do. Some may not have been as powerful or accurate as anticipated, but those problems required simple solutions.

This issue with the vines was that nothing worked, at all. We had tried fire, chemicals, saws, gunfire, explosives, even Axtin's hammer and Rokul's blades. The closest we had come was a small cut that was healed over soon after.

I sat in an empty office Rouhr had allowed for my use, contemplating my notes, when the door opened. I brought my eyes up to see the head guard. His mood was not pleasant, and I had an instant understanding of why.

"You were the one that brought her in, so she's your responsibility. If you don't come and deal with her, I'm letting her ass go, understand me? I'm not dealing with that damn woman, not for something as petty as stealing a goddamn vegetable." His basso was rich and vibrant, echoing off the walls of the empty office.

"An apple is a fruit according to the humans," I corrected. "Are you telling me that you and your men can't deal with one tiny woman?"

He snorted. "I'm telling you that me and my men don't *want* to deal with that tiny woman. She's an annoyance, and she's surprisingly good at insults. I've had to send one of my men home when he drew his weapon on her."

"Well, perhaps your man is ill-suited for his duties," I responded.

He shook his head in anger. "Don't. Don't lump yourself in with that woman by insulting my men. Come down and deal with her, or I'll let her go and whatever she does will be on your head, and your conscience, if you're who I think you are." With that, he spun on his heel and left, the door slamming behind him.

The notion that he would release Nesta in order to no longer listen to her was asinine. However, I knew that he was also a man of his word. He would release her if I did nothing.

Perhaps I should let her go, there was little real harm that she could do, and she was only stealing to survive. No. Stealing was wrong, and she shouldn't be allowed to continue living a life of crime. She had to know that there were consequences for her actions and that those actions needed to change.

I rose from my chair with a groan and made my way to the prison. I found myself dragging my feet, as the humans would say. I did not wish to confront her, simply because I had more important things to concentrate my efforts on. However, if I did nothing, she would simply return to her degenerate life of thievery that would eventually lead to her being killed by someone.

Why I cared about her well-being and life, I did not know, but I was soon at the jail. "Well, where is she?" I asked upon entering. I surprised myself a bit with the level of venom present in my voice. It worked, however, as the guard at the door directed me down the hall, through the second door, then to the fourth door on the right.

Upon my arrival at the fourth door on the right, I looked through the small barred window. Nesta had apparently convinced the guards to allow her a quick shower and I was able to finally see that her darkly colored hair was a natural color, not just dirt. Her skin, now clean, looked soft and smooth. She was lying on the bunk, her arms folded behind her head, a leg bent so the other leg could rest on it. The gleam in her eyes as she looked at me looking at her was filled with devious satisfaction.

I had the door opened and entered, hearing the heavy steel door clank shut behind me with a loud echo. "I was unsure as to how a small woman such as yourself could be so problematic, but you have apparently found a way."

Her smile spoke volumes. "Aw, you actually care."

"I do not see how my statement expresses care in any way," I responded to her statement.

She shook her head and waved my own statement off. "Not that. You showed up, just like I wanted you to. You care."

"I assure you, young lady, I do not care about your well-being," I said as I crossed my arms and leaned back against the door. "I am simply here because the guards have complained about your attitude and actions. I would suggest that you accept your fate and learn from it."

As I pushed myself away from the door and began to turn around, I heard Nesta get off the bunk. I turned, leaving only my shoulder available to her if she attempted to attack me. "You're not leaving me in here," she said, her eyes burning. "All I did was take a few fruits." Her voice was beginning to grow in volume and desperation. "You can't leave me in here just because of a few things to eat!"

In an attempt to maintain my calm, I closed my eyes, took a deep breath, and responded. "You committed a crime, it is as simple as that. Criminals should be..." I was unable to complete my statement as she threw her arms in the air and screamed at me.

"You sit up here, acting all high and mighty, thinking you're better than everyone else, and you don't have a single clue as to what is really happening around here. You think I wanted to steal?" she was soon directly in front of me, poking me in the chest as she spoke. "I stole because I had to, not because I wanted to. I need to eat. You don't look like you've ever gone hungry, so I don't expect you to understand. You're just a typical fat cat that already has everything. I doubt you even have a clue what it means to go hungry."

If she only knew. I could feel my ire growing as she ranted, but I did my best to remain calm. "Everyone has a choice. Instead of doing what was right and honorable, you instead chose to steal. Your actions are what brought you here."

"*My actions?!*" she screamed. "If you knew why I had to steal, you wouldn't be such an asshole."

Having been around the humans long enough to learn their vernacular, I knew what 'asshole' meant, and I didn't appreciate it.

"I don't care what your reasoning is," I yelled at her, my voice echoing off the walls. "You broke the law, you made a choice, you screwed up!" I took a deep breath and brought my voice back down to a normal volume. "You have no reason that will convince me that stealing was a necessity. You're nothing but a simple thief with no skills or abilities. You're a coward."

She tried to slap me, but I was prepared for it. I blocked her attempt and grabbed both of her wrists. I moved my face close to hers. "You have wasted enough of my time with your insolence and I will not stand for it. If I am called back in here to deal with you, I will forcefully remove you from here and throw you into the smallest, darkest, most forgotten cell available and forget that you've ever existed. When you're on the verge of starving to death, I'll come back, feed you, then force you to work until you break. Do you understand me?"

I should have known better than to get close to her. She swung her head forward, headbutting me in the chin. She laughed as I stumbled back, but I still had one of her wrists in my hand. I yanked her up in the air, shook her, and grabbed her. I walked her over to her bunk and slammed her down on it. "Don't make me come back."

"When can I get out of here?" she asked. "You can't lock me up indefinitely just because of a few apples."

Unfortunately, as much as I wanted to leave her to rot in here, she was correct. The penalty for stealing a few fruits was essentially a slap on the hand. She had already been in a cell much longer than she normally should have been.

"You need to make a change in your life. When you are capable of convincing me that you are ready to be a necessary and contributing member of society, I'll let you out. Until then, you stay…quietly," I said, making sure that the growl in my voice was enough to scare her.

"You're a dick," she spat at me. Not knowing what she had just said, I merely nodded and sighed.

"Very well. Enjoy your small accommodations, I'm sure your bucket will hold enough waste to prevent a mess in here," I indicated the small bucket in the corner. I walked away, the door closing behind me. Her curses chased me until I left the building.

NESTA

"Sylor is a dick!" I sang, banging my tin cup against the door. "Sylor is the king of dicks, and so say all of us!" I continued repeating my improvised verses for the good part of an hour, hoping that the guards would go crazy. It didn't take much longer before one of them was standing before my cell.

"Would you mind shutting up for a second?" he asked, looking at me through the small window, and I retreated a few steps to recline on the bed. This one was a Valorni, as well, and, judging by the expression on his face, he looked like he was nursing a headache. Mission accomplished. I'd had my doubts if those alien bastards could get headaches, but now I was sure of it.

"What? Don't like the song?" I asked politely, jumping off my bunk and heading toward the door. I offered him a polite smile and then bit the corner of my lip. "What's your name, guard?"

"It's Nover," he growled, massaging his temples.

"NOVER IS A DICK!" I started as loudly as I could. "NOVER IS THE KING OF DICKS, SO SAY ALL OF US!"

"For fuck's sake," he shook his head, stalking away from my cell to his post.

"Who taught you those bad human words?" I cried out, banging on the door with my cup. "Your mom would be disappointed!"

"SHUT UP!" he shouted, and I couldn't resist but shout right back at him.

"YOU SHUT UP, YOU GREEN BASTARD!"

This time, he was smart enough not to reply. He just sat at his desk, looking down at his datapad while he jammed his enormous thumbs inside his ears. That, of course, only made me bang louder. I only gave up when my arms started getting tired, and returned to my bunk to think of new verses for my song.

I had always liked being alone, but being in a prison cell was a totally different experience. I wasn't there of my own volition, and I had to depend on others to survive. If any of those bastards decided to starve me out, there'd be little I could do to stop them. I could sing louder, yes, but I figured that'd only piss them off more.

I remained in bed for the next few hours, occasionally practicing my song at the top of my lungs, and I only shut up when I started hearing voices outside. I climbed out of bed and immediately peeked out the window. My first thought was that the guards had complained to Sylor again, and that he was coming back to guilt-trip me again. I didn't exactly like him, but at least his presence distracted me from the bare walls I now had to call home.

Sylor was nowhere to be seen, of course, nor was Nover. He was in one of the adjacent corridors, apparently, and he seemed to be talking with one of the human guards. Humans sounded much softer than the Valorni, so it was easy to distinguish their voices.

"...a waste of time, really," the man was saying. "Sylor has been at it ever since the vines went crazy. And still, nothing."

"Sylor is smart," Nover replied, his tone harsh. "He's about the best weapons engineer we have. You'll see. He'll find a way to blow the damn things."

"Maybe it isn't a weapon we need," the other guy said, and I could almost imagine him shrugging by the tone of his voice. "I heard that the chemist we have working in the lab has some kind of toxin that works on the vines."

"A toxin," the Valorni snorted. "What we need is to blow through the vines, not give them medicine."

"A toxin isn't medicine," the man protested.

"Then why don't we use that medicine right now, huh?"

"The *toxin* we have isn't enough," the guy continued, correcting the Valorni dumbass. "Apparently, they only have half a vial, which is not enough to synthesize. They need more of it, but being that we're trapped inside the city—"

"Exactly," Nover cut the man short, his tone a triumphant one. "We have to go with an explosion. That toxin is a waste of time."

"Man, you Valorni really are thick."

"Yeah, they are," I finally joined the conversation, raising my voice. "Aside from creating useless weapons, there's not much they're good at."

"Don't you ever shut up?" Nover said, finally walking into view with his colleague, a lanky man with thin hair that didn't look older than thirty. There was a nametag on his uniform jacket, one that told me he was called Sam. "Are all women this annoying?" Nover asked.

"If you marry them, yes," Sam laughed, looking at me with a smug grin.

I was about to continue mocking those two when I remembered why I had joined the conversation in the first place. If Leena and Sylor were looking for a specific toxin, I knew exactly the place to go. The underground existed in more places than just Nyheim, and one of the underground marketplaces I knew was renowned for its unlicensed apothecaries, illicit substances traffickers, and all sorts of fun family-related activities. I was willing to bet that the toxin, whatever it was, could be found in such a place. Even if no one had the toxin, I was pretty sure I could find someone that would know where to look for it.

Now, if I could convince Sylor I could take him to the toxin...

"Get Sylor for me," I said to the two guards. "There's something I need to tell him."

"Get out of here," Sam laughed. "I've heard about you. I'm not going to fall for one of your pranks. If I get Sylor down here because of you, he's going to rip my head off."

"So what?" I snorted. "Your face needs to be rearranged anyway. Or could it be that you're keeping something valuable inside that skull of yours?"

"She called you stupid," Nover nodded sagely, probably proud that his limited knowledge of our language was enough to pick up on my sarcasm.

"You keep this up and I'll make sure you won't get fed for a week," Sam frowned, folding his arms over his chest. Employing my best diplomatic skills, I just gave him the finger.

"Get Sylor, dumbass," I repeated. "Because if you

don't, I can assure you...next time he sees you, he's going to rip your head off for real."

"Yeah? And why would that be?"

"Because I know exactly where to find that toxin of his," I grinned, enjoying the way both the man and the Valorni stared at me, surprise taking over their faces. "Now don't waste my time and go get Sylor."

"You little..." He trailed off then, and I could see that he was struggling with what to do next. Shaking his head, he raked one hand over his face. "Wanda!" he called out, and a few seconds later another guard appeared, this time a woman that couldn't be much older than me.

"Sir...?"

"Go get Sylor," Sam whispered begrudgingly. "Tell him our new prisoner has some information concerning the dome he might find useful. It's about the toxin."

"That wasn't so hard, was it?" I smiled, and then just blew him a kiss. Without waiting for his reply, I just kept my smug grin on and returned to my bunk.

Lying down, I laced my fingers behind my head and waited.

SYLOR

I was headed out for the testing site when a guard came running to get me. Apparently, communications were still problematic.

"Sir," she said as she attempted to catch her breath. "The prisoner wishes to speak with you."

"And?" I was not interested in speaking with her again. My connection to that woman was over, for all I cared.

She was barely able to hide her impatience, as well as her skepticism, as she spoke. "She claims to have information that is vital to our attempt to escape the dome."

This caught me by surprise. While it was no secret that we were attempting to find a way to escape, to hear that she had a potential plan had me intrigued. Of course, I was apprehensive, as well. This could all be a ploy to simply annoy me yet again. "Did she say what this information was?"

"Not exactly, sir," she said with a quick shake of her head. "But she did mention something about a toxin." That bit of news was a virtual slap in the face. How could she possibly know about the toxin? "Will you come to speak with her, sir?"

I stared at the guard for so long she became uncomfortable and began shifting her weight from foot to foot. I was unsure of the bit of information this guard had for me. Was Nesta telling the truth and she truthfully knew about the toxin, or was she playing games with me...again?

"Very well," I relented, with a tremendously deep sigh. I found myself more annoyed than anything, sure that this was just another game that I did not have time for. "Lead on."

With a nod, she turned sharply on her heel and led me back to the jail. I traveled through the second door, walked down the hall to the fourth door, and had it opened for me. Inside, standing next to her cot, Nesta seemed to be waiting for me. She seemed to perk up as I walked in.

"You're going to let me out of here, and you're going to let me out soon." The sense of accomplishment in her voice was almost entertaining. She truly felt as though she had something that would get her out of this small room.

Keeping my own amusement hidden, I put on a scowl. "I don't have time for games and lies. What information do you have?"

She grinned and folded her arms in front of her. "Maybe I won't tell you, with that attitude."

I shrugged, knocked on the door, and began to leave when the guard opened it for me.

"Wait. Please."

I smiled, winked at the guard, and stepped back into the room, the door closing again behind me. "Well?"

She sat down on her cot, all smugness out of her expression. "I overheard some of the guards talking about your attempt to get through the vines, and they mentioned something about a toxin that could kill plants."

While I wasn't happy to hear about our failed attempts being the talk of the town, I kept my face passive. "And?"

"I know where to find that toxin," she said.

"What makes you think we need it?" I countered as I attempted to keep myself calm. If she knew where to get more of the toxin we needed, we might have a chance to get out.

Here is where the smugness returned. "Oh, you're trying to be calm and not show any sort of emotion, aren't you? I'm going to assume, correctly I might add, that you're about to tell me that you don't need the toxin because you already have enough, aren't you?"

I paused and looked at her stoically.

"So what if I am?" I asked.

She chuckled. "Then why did your eyes light up when I mentioned that I could find more of that toxin?"

Skrell. She was right. No matter how passive I had been able to keep my face, I knew that if she had been watching my eyes, my emotions would have been plain. The idea that she knew where there was more toxin was something that we had to look into. This was something that needed to be pursued.

"Very well," I sighed. "You have information about the toxin, and you would be correct in assuming that we need it."

"Ha!"

I waved her enthusiasm off. "Tell me what you know."

"Well, like I said, I know where to get more of this toxin you need."

"Where?" I asked.

"Nuh-uh," she shook her head. "Not that easy. I want out of here."

"Give me the information I want, and we'll see if it's worth releasing you for," I said.

She shook her head again. "No. I get out, then you get the information. Besides, it's not here in Nyheim."

I did a double take at that bit of information. "Not in Nyheim?" She shook her head. "Then what good is your information? We can't get out, the toxin is needed so we can get out, but the toxin is outside…so, therefore, your information is useless, and you've wasted my time. Hope you enjoy being forgotten until we need to clean up your skeleton."

I turned to knock on the door. Behind me, I could hear Nesta jump to her feet and rush over. "No. I can get us out of town. I know a way."

I looked down at her, my face blank.

"I know a way out of town," she repeated quietly, her face staring up at mine, an almost pleading look in her eyes. "I swear."

"You know how to get out of town, out of the dome, and get the toxin we need?" I asked, looking for clarification.

She nodded vigorously. "If I can get you out of the city, take you to the toxin, and help you get it, I get released." It was her attempt at negotiation, and I had to say that her release would be a small payment for finding a way out and getting the toxin.

"Slight amendment to your suggestion," I said, a finger held up. "You show me how to get out of the city, help me get the toxin, bring it back, and if it works, we let you go. If it doesn't, at least you got to see the outside one more time."

"Whoa, so if it doesn't work, I stay in here?"

I shrugged. "Maybe. I need to run this past my commander, anyway, so I'll get back to you soon enough."

"I noticed you weren't completely prim and proper that time," she shot at me with some sass as I left the cell.

I took the suggested deal and information to Rouhr.

"Do you think she's telling us the truth?" he asked.

"I wish I knew, sir," I answered. "She did seem to be confident in what she was saying, so there may be a chance that she's right."

"What if she's not?" he countered.

"Do we have any other choices?" I asked. "I've tried eighteen different methods, nineteen if I include Rokul and Takar's burn and cut attempt, and each one has failed. This *could* be something that works."

He sat in his chair, his hands steepled in front of his face, and thought about what I had told him. If Nesta was correct, and she seemed confident enough in herself to believe that she was correct, this was the best chance we had of freeing ourselves from this creature's hold. She had, in a very unusual way, impressed me.

After a long time of thinking, Rouhr finally ran his

hands through his hair as he sat back at his desk. "Do you trust her?"

"No."

He nodded, then fluttered his lips as he blew out a breath. "If you feel that she is truthful, that she honestly can find a way out of the city and direct us to where the toxin is, then proceed. However," he added as I began to rise, "you just said that you don't trust her, correct?"

"Correct," I answered.

"Then find out where the toxin is. Find a way to make her tell you," he ordered.

"When she finds the way out of the city, I can put her back in the cell to investigate whether her claims are valid. When I return, we'll let her go free if she was telling the truth."

"Are you sure that isn't a bit harsh?" he questioned.

"Not particularly, sir," I said slowly. "However, if her information is correct…"

"Then you can signal us when you have the toxin and we'll release her," he interrupted. "You were the one that captured her in the act, you were the one that arrested her, you were the one that recommended the harsh sentence. I took your advice because you wanted her to learn a lesson, and you wanted her to change her ways."

I nodded in agreement. I had done all of that.

"Good," Rouhr said with a semi-evil grin. "Then you can determine when to release her."

"Yes, sir," I said, getting to my feet. Somehow, I truly felt bad for her. I was going to have to find a way to extricate the location of the toxin from her, then bring her back to her cell. I was not looking forward to her temper when that happened.

"Good luck," Rouhr said.

I nodded and gave a half-hearted salute as I left his office. This was going to be fun.

NESTA

"Oh, man," I said, stretching my back as I let a smile spread across my lips. "It feels good to be outside." Even though there wasn't any sunlight outside - the vines blocked it all - it still felt amazing to be able to walk more than five feet before bumping into a wall. The only thing that didn't feel amazing at all was the tall Valorni I had following me around.

Sylor wasn't really that bad, though.

His talk of justice and punishment made him slightly annoying, more so because it was exactly those stupid ideas of his that had landed me in jail, but he did seem to have his heart in the right place. His one purpose seemed to be the destruction of Nyheim's vine prison, and he seemed to want that because he was

genuinely worried about the people. Too bad his need
to help out involved putting people like me behind bars.

"Don't get too far," Sylor warned me, laying one his
hands on my shoulder and ensuring I wasn't more than
two feet away from him. "You're still a prisoner,
remember."

"Yeah, yeah," I sighed. "I know that."

"But if you're telling the truth, if there really is a way
out of the city..." He warmed up then, his usual grim
expression giving way to a thin smile. "Deliver on your
promises, and you might just find yourself a free
woman."

"Of course I'm telling the truth," I said, looking back
at him over my shoulder. "You might think I'm a thief,
but don't you dare think that I'm a liar. That's the one
thing I'll never do."

Of course, that was a lie.

When I told Sylor I knew of a way out of the city, it
really had been nothing but a calculated bluff. Sure, I
suspected there was a way out, but that was slightly
different than a full-blown promise. Still, I'd had no
choice: I had to remain out of that prison cell, whatever
the cost. If I remained locked up for nine months, away
from the underground, people wouldn't just resent me
like they do now. They'd consider me as an
outsider...and if I became an outsider, Sabre would
never be revived. And while at times I wanted nothing

more than to punch idiots like Topan and Stupid Joe in the face, they still were the only family I had.

"Alright, I'll trust you. You're not a liar," Sylor declared after almost a minute of silence, almost as if he had been weighing inside his head what I had just told him. "But why can't you tell me where we're going?"

"Because you wouldn't believe me," I grinned, glancing at him one more time. He narrowed his eyes at that, suspicious, but he still kept following me as I made my way through the maze of streets and alleyways in the Lua district. Most of the houses here were pretty much uninhabitable, vines as thick as a man jutting out from windows and rooftops, and most of the streets were completely deserted. It seemed that people had moved on from the district after the vines razed the place.

"In here?" Sylor asked, stopping as he eyed what was in front of us. It was a squat gray building, one that had been abandoned years before the Xathi had even set their sharp murderous feet on this planet. A local water treatment facility, it had become obsolete when the mayor went ahead with his plans to revamp the city's sewage system.

"Yup," I nodded, pushing on the rusty door with my shoulder. I groaned, struggling against the weight of the door, and then felt Sylor's hand on my shoulder once more. Carefully, he pushed me out of the way.

"I'll take care of that," he said, and then laid the palm of his hand against the door. One slight push and the damn thing quickly swung back on its hinges, slamming itself against the wall.

"Showoff," I grumbled, but Sylor just ignored me. He grabbed a flashlight from the tactical bag he had strapped to his waist and lit up the facility's inside. There were a few overturned metal chairs and desks, all of them covered with streaks of discolored rust, but aside from those things, there wasn't much to keep the eyes occupied.

"Follow me," I told Saylor, and then just stepped in. He ducked under the doorway, his movements wary, but didn't say a thing. Our footsteps echoed throughout the whole building, only growing mute when we went down a small ladder that gave access to an underground floor. The whole floor was nothing but a cramped little room, but it had the one thing I needed: a hatch that led straight into the underground tunnels.

"Do the honors, muscle-head," I said, pointing at the hatch. I folded my arms over my chest and let Sylor get to work. He kneeled right before the metallic hatch, laying his hands on the massive bars that served as a lock mechanism. I watched the muscles in his arms come alive, the purple bands that ran the length of his forearms snaking over his skin, and only when he finally opened the hatch did I realize I had been holding my breath.

"Is there something wrong?" he asked me, looking at me curiously. I felt warm blood rush to my cheeks, but just gritted my teeth and pretended it was nothing. Because it really was nothing, I tried to convince myself. Sylor could be an impressive specimen, sure, but that didn't mean anything.

"Yeah, there is," I smiled, now my turn to lay one hand on his shoulder. "You're in the way." He shifted back slightly, just enough to let me through, and I grabbed the handle of a creaky metal ladder that dove straight down into the darkness.

"I really hope you know what you're doing, Nesta," Sylor said, watching me as I started climbing down the ladder. I had both my feet on the floor even before he had finished speaking.

"Is the big Valorni scared?" I laughed. "C'mon, Sylor, don't be a pussy. Get down here."

"I find your vernacular speech inappropriate, Nesta," he protested as he started climbing down. I just raised both my eyebrows, hands on my hips as I watched him descend.

"My what?" I shook my head. "Sylor, you're the weirdest green dude I've ever met."

"I believe you," he said as he found his footing.

"Being that, in all likelihood, you haven't met many of my race, that's probably an accurate assessment."

"Never mind," I sighed, grabbing the flashlight from his hand and leading the way. We were in a small tunnel that was part of the old sewage system, and the ceiling was so low that Sylor had to walk in a crouch. We walked for fifteen minutes, and then our tunnel led onto another, and then another.

"What is that?" Sylor asked, pointing toward the light that finally appeared at the end of the tunnel. Smiling, I turned off the flashlight and threw it back at him.

"That, my green friend, is the underground," I proudly announced as we stood at the end of the tunnel, a cavernous hall right in front of us. Tents had been pitched as far as the eye could see, merchants plying their wares every step of the way, and loud voices bounced off the tall stone walls. The ceiling looked as if it was glowing a pale amber, industrial lights mounted in the stone at regular intervals. The spectacle paled in comparison to how the underground really was a few months ago, but it still felt good to be home.

Sylor was speechless.

"Cat got your tongue?" I asked him, feeling slightly amused at his reaction.

"What cat?" He narrowed his eyes in confusion, but

then just shrugged. "What is this place? And, more important than that, *how* is this place here?"

"Some of us don't like the surface," I shrugged as we started making our way through the cavern, a lot of curious eyes drawn by Sylor's towering presence. The only aliens most of these people had seen had been the Xathi, and they didn't have fond recollections of those. "C'mon, let's hurry up. There's a tunnel on the other side of this place."

"Nesta?" I heard someone call after me, and I froze on my tracks. I turned around to see Topan standing between two merchant stalls, the palm of his hand resting on the butt of a gun. Frowning, he pointed toward Sylor. "What the hell is this?"

"Let me speak with him," I whispered at Sylor, gently resting my hand on his forearm. Raising my voice, I turned back to Topan. "This is Sylor. He's not interested in the underground. He's just in here to assess the damage caused by the vines."

"Assess the...?" Topan trailed off, his jaw growing slack. "Are you out of your mind, Nesta? Why the hell would you bring one of these guys down here?"

"I did it because I had to," I replied, trying to sound as aggressive as Topan. "Look at the mess we're in. We survived the Xathi, sure, but these damn vines brought us down on our knees. This guy just came to see if he could help. Besides," I continued, already thinking of a lie, "the geologists on the surface think the sewage system might cave in at any given moment. And if that happens, we'll be trapped in here. And you know what that would mean for us all."

I held my breath then, hoping that my imaginary threat of being cut off from the outside world was enough for Topan to let this slide. He glared at me for a short moment, but then just shook his head and moved out of the way. "You're batshit crazy, Nesta. Has anyone ever told you that?"

"Only every day," I said, already moving past him. Sylor seemed as if he was about to say something, but I just dug my fingernails into his forearm, forcing him to shut up. He got the hint, thankfully, and only spoke up when we were out of earshot.

"That one," he started, "I don't like him."

"Topan's okay," I said. "He's just protective of this place. We've survived this far because we don't go around announcing ourselves to the world. Besides, this is our way of life. Topan would be crushed if that were to change."

"I see," Sylor replied. Then, as if remembering something, he continued talking. "Back there...you lied to him. I thought you never lied."

"And why would you think that?" I laughed, having no idea if he was being sarcastic. "This way," I continued, pointing toward a small tunnel entrance right ahead of us. I went inside it, grabbing the flashlight back from Sylor's hand, and we continued on our merry way into the bowels of the underground.

"Look," he stopped all of a sudden, pointing toward a small burrow in the rock. There was a pile of rubble near it, and some discarded pieces of clothing lay abandoned here and there. "Someone lived here."

"Yeah, I know that," I whispered, sadly eyeing the little burrow that used to be my home. "Never mind that, let's just go." With that, I continued toward the end of the tunnel. The ceiling grew lower with each step I took, and it didn't take long before I had to crouch. As for Sylor, he was almost on his hands and knees.

When I finally saw the wall of dirt that marked the end of tunnel, I prayed for fate to be kind to me. It was showtime. "Do you have a knife or something?" I asked him, and he grabbed one with a small but sharp blade from his bag. Using the tip, I started poking at the wall.

There was no stone there, and the earth was soft enough for me to start carving through it with just the blade. It only took me a few seconds before I revealed a few vines, these only as thick as my fingers. When I saw that they weren't packed as closely together as the ones on the surface, I breathed out with relief.

"See?" Turning back to Sylor, I handed him back his knife. "If I had to guess, the edge of the dome on the surface continues into the underground. Thing is, the vines seem frail in here, and they aren't that packed together. If we just push them apart, we can dig our way out."

"Not bad," he whispered, more to himself than to me. "Not bad at all."

SYLOR

I had to admit that I was pleasantly shocked. For a woman that I thought was simply lying though her teeth to get out of custody, she had managed to follow through on her claim.

She had found a potential way out.

This…underground city beneath the bones and skin of Nyheim was a wonder. The simplicity of things down here, combined with the desperation and resilience of the inhabitants, made for a place where I was sure people would grow to be strong, yet weak. I understood now why Nesta had stolen the fruits from the old woman…they would be worth much in a place such as this.

There was no fresh food, or at least, very little to be seen anywhere. These people were scavengers, hunters, and—for lack of a better term—inventors. They created and built what they needed to survive below the surface. They had dug tunnels where there weren't any, created homes where there shouldn't have been homes, and found a way to bring light and life to this... 'underground.'

Nesta was beaming with pride as I looked at the vines. "You did well, little one," I whispered as I studied the gaps in the vines. They weren't quite big enough for me to fit through, but with a little bit of effort and the proper tools, I could get through. "You did well."

Nesta smiled, and for the first time since our meeting, I felt that the smile was truly genuine, and mildly beautiful.

"We need to return to the surface to inform General Rouhr," I whispered. "We will also need tools."

"What do you mean, 'we'?" she whispered back.

I wasn't quite sure why whispering felt like the right thing to do, but it just was. I looked at her. "I will require your assistance. You brought me down here and I will need you to bring me again."

"Fine," she said, her voice rising in volume. "As long as you follow through on your end of the deal, I'll help you."

I nodded, knowing that the general had different plans for her. As she led me back through this underground world, I memorized the way, the locations of every turn, every corner, and every small change of direction.

Upon regaining the surface and allowing my eyes to readjust to the light of the city, it was time to get the equipment needed...and to put Nesta back within her cell. "Come," I said. "Let us get the tools that we need."

She nodded and followed me. It wasn't until we were close to the general's building that she began to hesitate. "Why are we going there?"

I looked back at her. "To get our tools, what else?"

"We couldn't get tools from somewhere else?" she asked.

"We may have been able to, but I am not familiar with everyone still within the city. I cannot simply take tools from people that I do not know," I answered her. Before she could speak again, I held up my hand. "And, no, to the best of my knowledge, we do not have stores of tools everywhere within the city. Our equipment is stored where we are and nowhere else."

She nodded, but she did not seem to believe me. She seemed to know that I wasn't telling her everything. Her trust in me, no matter how little it was before, seemed to be waning.

As we entered the building, I could sense that Nesta was even more uncomfortable. Her eyes darted back and forth, looking at everything she could. If she saw any of the guards that I knew were stationed in the building in certain secluded places, she would run.

Upon entering the building, I commented that our equipment was in one of the storage rooms in the basement. As I led her to the stairs, a guard sneezed.

She stopped moving. When I looked back at her, she looked like a feral animal trapped in a corner. Her eyes wide, her breathing heavy, she looked ready to run. "You're not letting me go, are you?" she whispered.

I spent half a moment choosing my words, but that was all she needed. With a snarl in my direction, she bolted. I dropped my head, glared at the guard that had sneezed, and chased after her. "Where are you going to go?" I called after her. She was a sprightly little one, but my much longer stride allowed me to keep up with her easily.

"Away from you, you lying bastard," she yelled back at me as she sprinted down the streets, dodging around people that struggled to get out of our way. "You lied to me. You were going to lock me back up!" she accused me.

"Not forever," I responded. "As soon as I found the toxin, I was going to call the general and he was going to release you."

"And you believed him?" she sounded incredulous, and out of breath. I truly had no idea where she thought she was going to go. The only place she could have gone to escape was underground, and I was certainly not going to allow her to get there.

"He's an honorable man. He would not go back on his word unless you gave him reason to," I explained as I loped behind her, allowing her to keep a short distance between us. People moved out of our way as she led us—purposefully? —away from the populated areas and into a park. It was an...interesting experience, watching her run. The way her body moved as she sprinted made me consider the possibility of how she would look and how well she would have been able to care for herself if she hadn't lived in the underground city.

"Liar! You lied to me," she continued to yell at me as we ran.

I was tired of this charade, and of being called a liar. While it wasn't too far from the truth, for I *had* lied to her, this entire scenario was becoming tiresome. It had to stop. As we raced through the park, I increased my pace a bit. As I got within a few feet of her, I dove, tackling her to the ground, twisting my body so that I took the brunt of the landing.

As she landed on top of me, my head came into contact with the ground under the thick grass. While it was not terribly painful, it was enough to cause my vision to blur momentarily. When my vision returned, I looked up into Nesta's eyes and noticed for the first time the small explosion of gold mixed in with the dark brown coloring.

Her breath came hard and heavy, her chest heaving against my own. I was suddenly aware of the shape and firmness of her breasts and the slight sweetness to her breath. Her deeply tanned skin, a mystery to me as the others in the underground were pale, complemented the green skin of my arms as I held her close.

Her voice, when she finally spoke, was soft and almost sultry sounding. "I'm not going back to that cell. You need me to find the toxin."

"Are you so sure of that?" I asked. We did have Jeneva to ask about the toxin, despite her current condition. She had dealt in the trade of toxins, plant materials, and other things during her time living on her own before we had arrived with the Xathi. She may have an idea of where to look.

Nesta nodded, which caused her body to shake against mine. The curves of her figure were certainly there. I could feel within my own blood a stirring of heat and pheromones.

"I know where to look," she said. "I can almost guarantee that you don't have anyone with a clue."

"You would be surprised," I countered. I enjoyed watching her eyes light up when she talked, subtly boosting her own value in order to persuade me to keep her around.

Her face seemed closer to my own. I looked at the shape of her lips, the tiny creases in them as she licked them nervously. I experienced an almost primal urge to bring those lips against my own.

She pushed herself away from me, settling herself tailor-fashion in the grass. "Fine, go without me. And when you fail, which you will, you'll take me out and have me show you anyway. Why not save yourself the trouble and just take me with you now?"

I sat up and found myself finding the feel of the grass very acceptable, though not as nice as Nesta's body against my own. "You're so sure of yourself," I stated, ensuring that it didn't come across as a question.

"I am," she nodded. "I promise you, you'll never find that toxin without me, and you and your people will be stuck in this dome until whatever made it decides what to do with you."

As much as I did not wish to admit that she was correct, she was. While she had shown me a possible way out, I was also fairly confident that the people down there would not take kindly to an entire team, or teams, or even an entire city of people invading their area in a desperate attempt to escape.

I laughed. There was nothing left to do but laugh. "Very well," I managed through a few chuckles. "You show me the way," then I put on a serious face. "But no running away. The creature that is responsible for these vines may very well decide that it is finished searching and it will then destroy the city, and that will include the people underground. We do this for everyone, not just ourselves."

She nodded.

I got to my feet and held a hand out for her to take. "Then let us gather our gear and find a place to sleep... not in a cell."

Her smile at those last four words was beautiful. Skrell.

NESTA

I opened my eyes lazily, enjoying the way the soft sheets had wrapped themselves around my body during the night. The place I was in was nothing but a modest bunk room, but it beat the jail cell I had been in before. Besides, I had the whole place to myself, and I even had an extra blanket, one I had made sure to throw over the sheets before I tucked myself in last night.

Sitting up on the bed, I finger-combed my hair as I yawned.

I had slept through the night like a rock and, for the first time in weeks, hadn't had any nightmares. I had never been prone to those, but after the Xathi had decided to pack their lunchboxes with some of my friends, a good night of sleep had suddenly become a commodity.

"Let's see," I whispered, swinging my legs off the bed. Still in my underwear, I padded my way across the room toward the door. I laid my hand on the handle and, trying to be as sneaky as I possibly could, I turned it. I cracked the door open, just enough so I could peek outside, but closed it the moment I saw the back of the guard Sylor had stationed outside the room.

That guy had trust issues, no doubt about it.

I was halfway through getting dressed when the door swung open all of a sudden. I turned around fast, clutching my blouse against my bare chest. "What the hell do you think you're doing?" I growled, shooting daggers at the confused Valorni standing by the doorway.

"I came to see if you were ready," Sylor said, and I couldn't help but notice the way his eyes were drinking in the shape of my figure. My heart sped up a little, and I felt warm blood rush to my cheeks. "Apparently, you're not."

"No shit, you genius," I said. "Now turn around and let me finish getting dressed."

"Right," he said, turning around but never leaving his place by the doorway. I was almost sure that he was feeling embarrassed he had caught me half-naked, but I couldn't really tell when it came to Sylor. He wore honesty and justice on his lapel, but his emotions...those he kept tucked away.

"I'm ready," I finally announced, slinging my backpack over my shoulder. When Sylor started turning, I was already walking past him and outside. "C'mon, let's not waste any time. Where do you have your tools?"

"This way," he said, leading the way through a maze of corridors. We ended up in what looked like an engineering shop, a few large tables lining the walls, dozens of soldering tools piled on their surfaces. There were at least two industrial presses in there, and small pieces of electronics littered the floor.

"Is this where you work?" I asked him, watching as he headed straight toward one of the tables and start packing up. He grabbed a few weird gadgets and, even though I had no idea what they were, I didn't ask. The only things I recognized were what seemed like a foldable drill and an old but reliable shovel.

"Yes, this is where I work," Sylor replied. He went down on one knee and then started making sure everything fit inside his large bag. "Not always, of course, but I do spend a lot of time in here. I like to build new things."

"Huh," I whispered, now glancing more attentively at what was on top of the tables. There were a lot of unfinished gadgets there, a lot of them suspiciously similar to weapons systems. I picked up a few of them, just to feel their weight, and couldn't stop myself from being amazed at Sylor's creations. Sure, I didn't know the purpose of most of them, but just the sheer quantity...he didn't like to build new things, he freaking *loved* it.

"Got your toys?" I asked him as he stood up.

"Not toys," he corrected me, "but yes, I do."

"Then let's get going."

We left the building then, Sylor carrying all the tools we would need while I ensured the only thing I had to carry was a bright green apple I had managed to steal from the officer's mess. I took a large bite out of it, moaning audibly as the apple's juice ran down my chin.

"What?" I asked Sylor as I noticed him looking, my mouth completely full.

"Nothing," he said. I wasn't sure if I was going mad, but I was almost certain there was a hint of a smile on his lips just then. He liked pretending he was this hardcore badass who built weapons and bombs for fun, but deep down, he was a softie. In a way, that almost made him endearing. *Almost.*

We made our way back to the underground unimpeded, and this time no one there questioned Sylor's presence. Topan gave us one of his annoyed stares but, in the end, he cared more about the underground's structural integrity than he cared about the fact my companion was a scary-looking green alien.

"How are the tunnels looking, Nesta?" he asked me, following after me and Sylor. "Will the sewage ones cave?"

"He can't know where we're going," Sylor told me under his breath. "I don't want any civilians following us. No one gets out before we know if it's safe. I'll post guards down here if I have to."

"No need for that," I pushed past my gritted teeth, already annoyed at Sylor's suggestion. Topan and the old gang would hate my guts if more Valorni started coming down here...especially Valorni that used such nefarious titles as guards. "Sylor just wants to check on a few more things," I told Topan, lying through my teeth. "We'll be out of your hair soon enough, don't worry."

"You're pretty good at lying," Sylor told me as we left Topan behind and entered the tunnels that went past my old burrow and toward what I hoped to be our digging site. "I hope you're not lying to me right now, Nesta. This city really needs that toxin."

"I might be a liar, but I'm not a dickhead like you," I protested. "I know the city is screwed without that toxin. And these people..." I gestured toward the cavern we had just left. "They are *my* people. I want to protect them, too, believe it or not."

"*That* I believe."

"Good," I said, fishing another apple from inside one of my pockets. I was so busy with digging my teeth into it that I didn't even notice Sylor had stopped right in front of me, and so I just crashed against him. "What the hell, man?"

"We're here," he said, awkwardly turning back to face me. The ceiling was so low he couldn't stand up, and even I had to crouch slightly. He got to work almost immediately, unpacking his bag and laying all the tools on the floor right in front of him. He picked out a small, round, flat gadget, and pressed it against the wall in front of him.

"What are you doing?"

"This is a kind of sonar," he explained. "It'll allow me to see what lies ahead of us." Pushing a button on the circular gadget, he closed his eyes. At the same time, the purple bands on his arm lit up. I took a step back, surprised, but quickly realized what was happening. The lights on his prosthetic sleeve were activating.

I could see Sylor's eyes moving rapidly under his eyelids, matching the rhythm of his glowing bands. Somehow, the small gadget he was using was transmitting all the information into Sylor's bionics.

"Nice," I nodded approvingly. "Didn't know you were that handy."

"That's because you weren't paying attention," he

said, this time with a smile. That was witty of him. Taking into account that most times he seemed to talk as if he were reading a textbook out loud, I couldn't help but be impressed. "Now, I've scanned the earth in front of us, and it seems you were right. We can push our way through the vines, since there are only a few of them here...then we'll tunnel forward until we find bedrock, and only then will we start digging upward."

"Sounds like you have it all figured out."

Using his shovel, he then busied himself with loosening the layer of earth right in front of him. He uncovered the vines that crawled up toward the surface and, holding on to them, started pushing them apart. The muscles in his shoulders bulged from the effort, and I didn't even pretend I wasn't staring. Sylor's body was more than just impressive...it was as if someone had designed it with perfection in mind.

"Good enough," he announced as he grabbed his drill. Going down on one knee, he unfolded it and then set it up, pushing the tip against the earth. It whirred loudly as it dug deep into the wall, and piles of dirt started accumulating at his feet. "You wait here," he told me after he had carved up a nice burrow, one large enough for him to squeeze inside, although with a lot of difficulty. As far as I was concerned, that little tunnel looked uncomfortably tight. "I'll call you if it's safe."

With that, he continued pushing his way deep into

the earth and, after half an hour, I could no longer see him. I just heard the perpetual sound of his drill and his occasional groan. I stared down the cramped little tunnel Sylor had managed to create, and I felt my heart starting to beat anxiously. I couldn't help but anticipate the moment I would have to follow after Sylor, the walls closing in on me, the air becoming more and more rarefied...

"Snap out of it, Nesta," I told myself, but the darkness in front of me wasn't helping matters. It was odd for an underground woman like me to be afraid of tight, cramped places, but I had never really managed to get those fears under control.

Not after what Odeon, my mentor, had done to me.

"You can come now, Nesta!" Sylor called me.

I remained frozen in place, not moving an inch. I looked at the small tunnel in front of me, and then I looked back to the way we had come. I could run now and, in the tunnels, there was no way Sylor would ever find me. I didn't need to crawl inside that dark tunnel, did I?

I could just turn around, leave...

I'd be free once more.

"Nesta?" Sylor insisted. "Are you there?"

"Coming!" I shouted back.

Shutting down my rational mind, I bit the bullet and crawled into Sylor's tunnel.

SYLOR

The way in front of me was just rock. None of my tools would be capable of getting through that, not in the small space that we had to work with. I had made it a point to try to dig the tunnel out to at least one and a half times my size in order to allow myself a little bit of room to work with, as well as room to push the dirt out behind me as I dug it out.

Now, it was time to dig upward and hope that my excavations resulted in an escape from the vines. As I lay on my back, I looked down towards my feet at Nesta, who looked to be sweating. "How are you doing?" I asked her.

She looked up at me, swallowed, and nodded. "I'm okay. Not a fan of being in this tiny hole," she said through a forced chuckle. "Are we going any further?"

"In a fashion," I said. "I can't go any further forward, it's all rock." I tapped the rock wall behind my head in emphasis. "I'm going to have to start digging upwards."

"That should be fun," she teased. Her humor sounded forced, but I attributed it to her just being cramped in this small tunnel. Perhaps 'cramped' was the wrong word. She was much smaller than me, so perhaps she was just not keen to be in a tunnel with tons of loose dirt hanging over her head. I had to admit that I was a bit apprehensive with the concept myself.

"I'll do my best to move most of the dirt towards you as I'm drilling and digging, if you wouldn't mind helping to keep me from burying myself," I said with a grin. She looked so uncomfortable, I had hoped that a grin would help ease her troubles.

It didn't seem to work. She nodded and waved at me to continue. With a short moment spent contemplating her well-being, I maneuvered myself a bit to the side, grabbed my small portable drill, and began drilling upwards. It was short work drilling up, the ground was much softer and easier to get through. The portion of the work that slowed me down, however, was the dispersal of the dirt. Nesta did a magnificent job of moving the dirt away from me and out of the tunnel as I continued to dig and drill my way upwards.

I reached a point where it was safer to use my shovel than my drill. The drill was too powerful for the loose dirt and rocks and I did not want to cause a cave in and bury myself under thousands of pounds of earth.

Three minutes after switching to the shovel, dirt began falling faster and faster. Soon, I was being buried under a minor avalanche of soil, rock, and bone.

Nesta let out a small shriek as I turned my head down and scrambled away. After nearly a minute of cave-in, it finally stopped. I spat dirt from my mouth and shook it from my face and hair. I looked up to see Nesta wide-eyed and shaking. "Hey," I said, reaching out to touch her shoulder. "Just some loose dirt," I coughed. "It's…it's okay."

I coughed up more dirt and had to shake my head to clear the dirt that had fallen into my eyes. I could imagine how I looked, and it must have been terribly funny for Nesta was slowly letting a smile creep on her face as she attempted to hide her mirth.

"Dirt on my face?" I asked.

She nodded and failed to hide her smile and laughter as she pointed at my hair. "There's…there's some bone in your hair…right there."

I felt along my head and found several pieces of bone along the left side. I picked it out and tossed it to the side. "Well, that was fun," I laughed.

The smile left her face and the almost wild-eyed look returned. "Are you okay?" she asked me.

I nodded in answer.

"Do we keep trying?" she whispered, a slight tremble to her voice.

I nodded again. "I'm not sure how much further we have to go, but we need to finish. It's important."

"Okay," she mouthed. I repositioned myself so we could move the dirt away. After a few minutes of clearing the dirt, I was able to stand up and begin digging again. I slowed myself down to make sure that every bit of dirt I brought down was only the dirt I wanted to fall.

I got to a point where I was stretching to my limit, unable to get any higher. I tried to jump up and hold myself against the walls of the tunnel, but the soil was too loose. It didn't hold me, and I dropped to the ground, more soil raining down on my head. I shook the dirt off and looked at Nesta. "Well, I think we have to do something different." I took my drill and began drilling into the rock wall next to me.

After nearly fifteen minutes of drilling different points, I had several foot-holds. I climbed up, using a small piece of protruding vine to hold myself in place. Pushing with my left arm while bracing with my legs, I held myself in place. I pulled up my shovel and started digging slowly.

Within another half hour of digging, there was suddenly a stream of light coming through. I had reached the top. The elation I felt was...uplifting. I quickly opened the hole and peeked through the opening. We were out.

I looked down. "Nesta?" There was no answer. "Nesta?" I bent myself down to the best of my ability considering the small space. I saw Nesta's feet, but I was unable to see the rest of her. I carefully dropped down to the floor of the tunnel.

Nesta was on the ground, curled up in the fetal position, shaking. I knelt down next to her. "Nesta? What's the matter? What's going on?" I continued to speak to her, trying to get her to answer me, to respond in some way, but she stayed there, curled up and shaking.

I wasn't sure what else to do. I couldn't leave her there, but I was unsure of how to help her. I wasn't even sure as to what was bothering her and caused her to be this way.

I looked back down the tunnel, but it was nearly forty feet to try to drag her back through, and I couldn't vouch for how the inhabitants would react to me bringing her out of here in that manner. The only other option was to take her up and out of the tunnel, out into the open spaces of the outside.

I rushed back to where the tunnel turned up, climbed my way back up and quickly dug out the rest of the opening. I spent an extra minute enlarging the hole, then dropped back down. I wasn't entirely certain as to how I would get her out.

"Nesta?" I shook her. No response.

I thought about my options again. Back through the tunnel was bad—we would still be underground, and it would take me nearly an hour to get her back above ground. I had to get her up the tunnel and out. I would be able to see what had happened to her in the daylight, the light in the tunnel was too dim for me to see anything.

I picked her up, slung her over my shoulder and headed to where I could climb. I steadied myself as best I could and slowly, oh so slowly, began my climb. Two steps up and Nesta began to slip from my shoulder. I shifted her back up, took a moment to catch my breath, and attempted the climb again.

The burning in my shoulders, my elbows, and my legs was excruciating. My arms were shaking trying to hold us up. While Nesta was not particularly heavy, she was deadweight on me, and that deadweight was holding me down.

I reached up for a handhold, grabbed it, and it fell away. I slipped and Nesta fell from my shoulder and into the crook of my arm. The only thing holding us up was my legs and a vine that I had managed to grab. My breath came in quick bursts as I tried to shift her back up.

After what felt like ages, I managed to get her back up. I pulled on the vine, felt it begin to move, and pulled as hard and fast as I could. As the vine ripped from the surrounding tunnel wall, I let go and reached up. I caught onto the top edge of the tunnel, gripped a thick clump of grass, and held on for dear life.

It held.

It held and I pulled myself up, shifting Nesta to a point where I could begin to push her out. I pushed her up, my arm shaking, my shoulder burning from the exertion. With one final effort, I shoved her as hard as I could out of the hole and pulled myself up after her.

I laid in the grass, relishing the fresh air and the beating heat of real sunlight upon me. I rolled over to look at Nesta and was relieved to see that she was still breathing.

I laid back down, closed my eyes, and let a laugh escape my lips. We were alive, and more importantly, we were *out*. We were outside the dome. Even if we were unable to defeat the vines, we had a way out. There was a way out of our prison.

"Sylor?"

I opened my eyes to see Nesta sitting up, her face blocking the light of the sun. "Hi," I said quietly.

She fell on top of me, hugging me and thanking me for saving her. I hesitated a second, then hugged her back. "It's okay. We're out. We're out," I said, a smile spreading on my face as I said the words.

NESTA

I sat down on the grass near Sylor, and took a few deep breaths. My head was still spinning, my heart was beating at a thousand miles per hour, and even my vision was blurred. I felt the blades of soft grass under the palms of my hands, and I focused on the sensation to regain some semblance of control.

"Nesta..." I heard Sylor call after me, his voice sounding as if it were coming at me from the other side of the planet. "Are you okay?"

"Yeah..." I panted. I tried to look at him and smile, but even the slightest movement of my head was enough to make me nauseous. Looking down, my head tucked between my knees, I sucked in a deep breath and closed my eyes. "Just...just give me a moment. I'll be fine."

Sylor didn't say anything and, for that, I felt thankful. I heard him stand up, his heavy boots crunching the packed earth and grass under them, and realized he was already checking out the perimeter. Always aware, always cautious.

"Get ahold of yourself, Nesta," I muttered under my breath, running one hand through my hair. I wasn't even surprised when I noticed locks of hair were plastered to my face, sweat still running down my cheeks. At least I wasn't hyperventilating anymore. Both my hands were still shaking, though, and I had to use all my willpower to stop the rest of my body from shaking too.

Own your fears, I heard a voice say from deep inside my mind, one that drifted out from the vault of memories I had been keeping hidden away. It was raspy and strong, a hint of condescension hiding behind the words.

Odeon's voice.

I remembered the rigorous training he had put me through, and all the bruises my body collected whenever I failed to do whatever he wanted. From memorizing all the hidden routes that connected the different cities, to simple sleight-of-hand tricks I needed to master in order to become a successful member of Sabre, Odeon had been an unforgiving mentor.

I had been just a bony child when he took me under his wing, his smart and cunning eyes going hand-in-hand with his alluring promises of a full belly and a warm bed to sleep in. Relentless, I met each and every one of his challenges and lessons, and it didn't take me long to become his second-in-command. He had never made it official, since I hadn't been older than sixteen at the time, but by then I was pretty much running the majority of Sabre's operations.

I was Odeon's ideal student and, in due time, I would be Sabre's leader.

There was just one lesson I had never quite mastered...

Own your fears, his voice came again, and with it the sound of a key turning inside a lock, a metallic bolt falling in place with a deafening sound. I couldn't have been older than ten. I was small, but the closet Odeon had locked me in didn't have enough space for me to stretch my legs. I had to keep my head tucked between my knees, my elbows and feet pressed against the cramped walls that imprisoned me. I couldn't even move my head, and every breath I took hurt, as it expanded my ribcage and made the closet one size too small for me.

Odeon kept me locked in that closet for three days.

I didn't say a word back then, nor did I cry. Had I cried for help, Odeon would've just kept me locked in there for weeks. So I just braved it out. Somehow, I survived the ordeal...and at the time, I thought that would be it. Just one more challenge I had overcome.

Then came the nightmares.

I dreamt of being buried alive, of walls closing in on me, tightening around my body so much that I couldn't even draw a breath. The underground was my home, but Odeon had turned me into a claustrophobic.

"Hey, hey," I heard Sylor say right beside me. "It's okay, Nesta. I'm right here." He draped one arm over my shoulders, pulling me against his body, and only then did I realize that tears were streaming down my face. I gritted my teeth hard to stifle a sob, but rested my head against Sylor's chest all the same. His presence felt reassuring, and the sound of his beating heart somehow soothed me.

"Thank you," I whispered, wiping the tears off my face with the back of my hand. I took a deep breath, raked my hand over my face, and forced a smile upon my lips. Pushing myself off Sylor, I looked straight into his eyes. He returned my gaze, his expression one of concern, and I found all the fear I had felt before vanishing.

I didn't know what it was about Sylor, but I felt safe around him. He was my captor, the one that had put me in this stupid situation of having to save the city, and still...I couldn't help but feel this damned connection with him. Was that the reason why I had followed him this far? I could've left him behind, back when we were at the tunnels...and yet, I hadn't.

"Much better," Sylor whispered, his soft smile drawing my eyes. Reaching for me, he stroked the skin under my eyes with his thumb, wiping my face of whatever tears remained there. I felt my heart skip a beat as I felt the touch of his skin on mine, and my eyes were immediately drawn again to the way his lips were slightly parted...

I held my breath then, and the world stood still.

Then, when his eyes fell on my lips, a wave of embarrassment crashed against me. What the hell was I doing? Why was I feeling so damn vulnerable around him? No, I wouldn't allow myself to be that kind of person.

"So," I said, looking away from him as I cleared my throat. "It's a long way to Duvest. We should get going soon."

SYLOR

To have seen her panic, to have been reminded of pieces of my past because of it, I better understood her now. I hazarded a guess that, since she had grown up in the underground, she had been used to the standard-sized tunnels and warrens that were under the city, but when she had gotten into the smaller tunnel, something had gone wrong and brought her to that level of panic.

Now I understood her shaking and hesitation when we were digging our way out, and I better understood how much effort she had put into helping me, in guiding me, in staying with me long enough to find a way out. The respect that I had slowly been gaining for her due to her unending perseverance and unrelenting drive had increased a hundredfold now that I knew she had pushed herself as far as she had in order to aid me.

She had come to me for comfort after our escape and had placed herself in my care long enough to tell me what she was afflicted with, what it was that had caused her to fall into a panic. Now, I felt as though her protection was even more my responsibility than before. She would need me, and I was determined to be there for her.

During my times in the war against the Xathi, I had seen many a warrior, many a hardened soldier, come to be the same as Nesta was in the tunnel. There were many times that the battle, the war, the death and destruction, had come to be too much for someone. The panic that raged with a soldier's mind overwhelmed them, made them ineffective.

There were many within the military that branded those men as cowards, but I knew better. I had seen my own atrocities during the war, even committed some of my own against the Xathi, convincing myself that they were not truly such atrocities because the Xathi were mindless beasts.

Not everyone was born with a similar constitution, some were stronger than others. I had been lucky enough to have been born a very strong individual. I had been able to withstand seeing what I had seen thanks to training from both my father and my commanders.

Nesta, I assumed, had no such training, no such upbringing. She had grown up in a place that looked as though the people had all they could do to survive, for that was all there was, survival. There was no chance to thrive, no chance to become stronger, better, smarter, and to find a way into a better life. There was only survival, and if you couldn't survive until the next day, you were left behind. And something had happened to Nesta down there that had created this feeling of panic within her. I wanted to know about it so I could better help her, but I also knew that I could not ask, that if a person was ready to speak about their problems, they would be the one to begin discussing it.

Since she had not volunteered to do so, I knew she was not yet ready. "So," I started as we both sat on the grass. "Why Duvest?"

I could see the relief on her face. She had apparently been expecting me to ask about her condition. A light smile played on her face as she answered me. "Duvest has a special sort of marketplace where we can get the toxin, hopefully."

I was a bit confused. "I'm not sure if you would know this, but Duvest was damaged quite badly during the final Xathi confrontation, as well as the initial attack from our friend here," I explained, as I slapped my hand on the outside of the vined dome.

I got on my comm and signaled General Rouhr.

I advised him of our status.

"Proceed with the rest of your mission then, Sylor," he said to me. "And good luck."

I grunted and looked over at Nesta.

She flashed me another smile. "I know, but this little market will still be there...I think." Her confidence was bewildering, but I wasn't going to complain. If she was certain that the market was still there and we were still going to find the toxin, I was not inclined to complain. "Come on," she motioned to me as she got to her feet. She held out a hand, and I took it. While she wasn't strong enough to pull me to my feet, I certainly appreciated the gesture.

I showed her the direction we had to take in order to reach Duvest, and she took the lead. After nearly a mile of following one of the more well-used trails, Nesta took us off the trail. I struggled to see the reasoning behind it, but we had switched to what looked to be a tiny animal trail, barely cut through the forest floor.

"Why are we taking this pathway?" I asked her as I stepped over a fallen moss-covered log.

She looked back at me and winked. I felt myself mesmerized by her. She was certainly different than

any of the other human women that had been part of our dealings. As we continued walking, she pointed out several small little pods that were hanging from trees or protruding from other plants. "Do you see these? Don't touch them, not unless you have to," she cautioned.

"Why not?" I asked. I studied one of the pods a little closer. It was small, half the size of my foot, and they came in various colors. Some were green, others brown, and still others were a sort of purple color. Each had a tendril attached to it that pulsated every few seconds.

"They emit a sort of gas, or repellent, to keep predators away." She came over and pointed at one. "You see how their tails contract like that?"

I nodded.

"If it gets faster than that, then it's either feeling threatened and about to spray, or it's getting close to full and about to spray." She grabbed my arm and gently pulled me away. "Either way, it's a stink that will stay with you for months."

"That bad," I commented, my eyes a bit wide in wonderment.

She nodded. "Mm-hmm. If they spray due to a threat, there's a little something added into it that makes it burn. I've been lucky, but I knew people that weren't so lucky. Scars pretty bad, too," she added as she led the way.

"Is it really that bad?" I asked as I followed her down the trail.

"I've used them to keep people off my tail before," she admitted.

Impressive. "Really? So why aren't these trails used more often?" The fact that I had never seen these pods on the main trails, the main roads, suggested that the pods were much more comfortable in seclusion than in the open.

Nesta essentially mirrored my thoughts. "The trails are generally only used by those of us that know about them and want to stay away from others. The pods are sort of the same. They're only on these small animal trails, from what I've seen."

"No one else knows about these?" I asked.

She shook her head as she ducked under a low-hanging branch. I, however, wasn't as nimble, or small enough to simply duck. I was forced to get down on my hands and knees and crawl underneath. As I gained my feet, I looked up to see Nesta laughing at me. "What?"

She shook her head. "It's fun to watch you have to crawl when I can just duck. Guess that's your punishment for being so big and tall."

"Yes," I responded. "Now, what about my question?"

"What question?" she asked me.

I let out a soft snort. "The one where I asked if

anyone else knows about these," I said, indicating the trail with a wave of my hand.

"Oh," she shrugged. "Lots of people know about them, but not the people you're probably thinking of. If you're wondering if 'normal' people," she made an air-quote motion with her hands, "know about these trails, I'm going to assume that if they do, they don't use them because they're scared to use them. They're not big, they're not well-traveled, so they're most likely not safe to the general public."

I had to admit that her answer seemed the most plausible. A regular person would most likely look at the tiny animal trail and bypass it because it was so small. Most people were much more willing to take the well-used path than the new one that no one knew about.

Nesta and the people that she lived with were interesting people. They had chosen to live underground, below the city, and scrounge and scrap their way through life. Instead of coming above ground to live, they came above to get what they needed in order to survive. It bewildered me as to why they would choose to live that way.

What had driven them below ground in the first place? What had caused these people, several generations strong, to take themselves beneath the city to live? I understood, partially, why Nesta and her generation, as well as the younger ones, stayed; they knew nothing different, nothing better.

Apparently, they did come above ground, but none of them...maybe a few...chose to stay above. They always returned to the underground lives that they had known.

Nesta was an enigma, someone that confused and confounded me. She was strong, mentally, and stubborn. She was resourceful, confident, and—to a degree—arrogant.

She was also underfed, unprepared, and unable to properly care for herself.

I found myself struggling to keep my mind on anything other than her. She was a mystery that I was desperate to solve, and from our two brief moments of closeness, a mystery that I wanted to know everything about.

She seemed to be in her element out here, in the forest, more so than she was when she was leading me about in the underground. I wondered if I would be able to convince her to stay above when all of this was finally finished.

NESTA

"There," Sylor said, pointing into the distance. "The walls, can you see them?"

Using my hands to shade my eyes from the sun, I peered into the distance and, just like Sylor had said, the walls of Duvest rose up from the ground in all their majesty. Their bland surface contrasted with the lush green from the forest, marking the start of more civilized grounds.

"I see it," I finally replied. Walking faster now, I led the way down the small hill we were on, twigs and low-hanging branches whipping at my shoulders as we went. Sylor followed me closely, making so much noise that there was no doubt in my mind every creature in a five-mile radius knew exactly where we were. His body was powerful, yes, but it sure as hell wasn't built for stealth.

"What the hell happened here?" I said as we closed in on the city. The protective walls of the northwest district were riddled with holes, and the watchtowers had all crumbled, large blocks of granite lying abandoned on the ground. To cover up the holes in the walls, wooden palisades had been erected.

"I told you," Sylor said. "Duvest fell during the war. The city you knew...it's gone now."

He was right. I knew Duvest as a metropolitan city, one brimming with hopeful merchants and people trying to make their way through life, but the city in front of me was nothing like that. Aside from the few human guards patrolling the perimeter, there didn't seem to be much activity.

"Hold it!" One of the guards shouted as he saw us approach. Climbing down from the makeshift watchtower he was in, rifle slung over his shoulder, he then made his way toward us.

"At ease, soldier," Sylor said, completely relaxed. "We're just passing through. We need to pick up something from the city, and we'll be on our way."

"I'm not sure what it is you think you're going to pick up in here," the guard said, pointing with his thumb to the crumbling walls behind him. "But suit yourself. The Valorni are friends of the Duvest people."

He eyed me for a moment, but didn't say a word. Apparently, the fact that I was Sylor's companion was enough for the guard to wave me in. I liked that: to an extent, Sylor was my all-access pass.

"Thank you, soldier," Sylor said, and then we followed after the guard as he led the way toward the main city gate. He shouted someone's name, both hands around his mouth to amplify his voice, and I immediately heard a metallic rumbling sound. A second later and the gate was being heaved up by unseen hands.

"Enjoy your stay," the guard said, casually whistling as he returned to his watchtower.

"They don't seem too concerned with security," I told Sylor as we stepped inside the city. Ruins flanked the main avenue on both sides. Piles of rubble had accumulated on the sides of the road, as well, probably part of the cleanup effort. Still, Duvest looked like shit. The Xathi bastards had really outdone themselves here.

"Now that the Xathi are gone, everyone's feeling more relaxed," Sylor explained. "Besides, it's not like there's a lot to protect in the city. Almost all civilians have left. This place is just a ghost town."

"That's depressing."

"I know," he nodded. "Still, General Rouhr has plans for the city. As soon as we manage to liberate Nyheim, the plan is to start rebuilding Duvest. Hopefully, in a couple of months the people will return here, and life in Duvest will go back to what it once was."

"I seriously doubt that," I whispered, even though deep down I hoped Sylor was right. But a war left more than just ruins in its wake: some scars remained hidden from sight, and it'd take more than a decade for the wounds to finally start healing.

"Where to?" Sylor asked me, and I took a moment to orient myself. The fact that the streets were practically deserted was a shock, and I was having a hard time reconciling the Duvest I knew with the one I was in right now. "Another water treatment facility?" he offered.

"No," I shook my head. "Not in Duvest. In here, we usually go through an old factory," I continued, suddenly remembering where I had to go. Navigating the maze of streets more easily now, we made our way to the small industrial area Duvest had always been proud of, and pointed toward a dilapidated building right at the end of the road we were on. The war against the Xathi didn't seem to have affected it, but the building still looked like shit, all the same. Moss covered large sections of the wall, and grass was already jutting out from the pavement right in front of the entrance. The windows were all gone, and only one door remained, although it hung limply from half its hinges.

"The underground people should really invest in landscaping," Sylor commented, and I punched his arm playfully.

"Really funny," I said, already stepping inside the building. It was completely empty, aside from some broken glass that littered the floor. It seemed that even the few things that had been bolted to the floor had been taken away. No surprise there: whatever the underground people could take, they *would* take.

With Sylor trailing after me, I made my way toward the basement floor, the one used by the maintenance engineers when the factory was still in operation. There, I headed straight toward the control room that housed the main water valves. "Flashlight," I asked, and Sylor placed it my hand. I turned it on, shining some light into the maze of pipes that snaked across the room, and immediately spotted the large hole someone had made in one of the walls.

"Now it's just a short hike through one of the tunnels," I said, examining the hole in the wall with the flashlight. It was large enough for Sylor to fit through, and it seemed clean enough to indicate that, even after the war, people had been coming in and out of Duvest's underground.

Just like I had predicted.

We spent the next ten minutes walking down the tunnel, and we only stopped when we heard the sound of footsteps right ahead of us. Then, all of a sudden, a large figure emerged from the shadows and stood right in front of us. He was a human male and, even though he was smaller than Sylor, he was large enough to be intimidating.

"Who comes there?" he snarled, drawing a gun from his holster. He didn't point it at us, so I took that as a good omen.

"Calm down," I said, stepping forward and lowering my flashlight. "We don't want to cause any trouble. We're just on our way to the market."

"With one of those things?" the man asked me, eyeing Sylor as he spoke. As his eyes met those of the Valorni, I noticed his fingers tightening around his gun. Crap. "If you know of the market, then you can go through. But he has to stay. No way am I going to let one of those things through."

"He's not a thing," I found myself saying, annoyed by the man's tone. Still, he held the power in this situation. I couldn't start arguing with him. Of course, I wasn't worried about him stopping us...with Sylor by my side, I was pretty sure we could simply force our way into the underground. But I didn't think knocking out one the sentries would help our cause. "He's a Valorni, and he's my bodyguard."

"Hired muscle, huh?" the man said appraisingly, looking at Sylor as if he was examining some wild animal. "He does look scary, I'll give you that. Does he speak?"

I noticed Sylor was about to open his mouth, so I stomped on his foot. "Just a few words," I said with a smile. "He's not that talkative."

"Look, I get it. Having a bodyguard is a good idea if you can afford it," the man continued. "But I can't let him get to the underground. People could freak out, and I'm really not in the mood for that."

"What's your name?" I started, trying a different approach.

"Warren."

"So, Warren...am I supposed to tell Odeon you forced me to leave my bodyguard behind? This guy here," I said, patting Sylor's arm, "is with me because Odeon ordered it."

"Odeon?" He hesitated for a moment, and I knew I had him. Odeon's name was a powerful one in the underground, no matter what city you were in, and I was quite happy the news of his death hadn't travelled this far. I felt bad about using the old man's name like this, but it wasn't like I had a choice. Besides, it wouldn't make a difference for the bastard, him being dead and all. "Who are you, exactly?"

"The name's Nesta" I said, folding my arms over my chest and pretending I was growing irritated. "Let's leave, Sylor. It's pretty clear this guy doesn't want us to get to the market."

"Hold on!" Warren cried out. "I've heard of you, Nesta...and if this is what Odeon wants, then who am I to stop it?"

"Good thinking," I grinned, holding Sylor's arm as we passed through the sentry point. Sighing, he just leaned against the wall and holstered his weapon.

"Good work," Sylor told me the moment we were out of earshot. "You can think fast on your feet."

"Of course I can," I said with a smile, feeling more than just a little proud. As promised, I had sneaked Sylor out of Nyheim, and I had brought him to Duvest. Now, only one thing remained.

We had to find the toxin.

SYLOR

To say that I was confused and surprised would be akin to saying that the *Vengeance* was a cargo vessel.

The idea that there was yet another underground city blew my mind. The people of this planet knew nothing of their own kind, or of their own homes. She had walked me into a building as simple as anything and brought me through a small passageway down to this city.

This underground city that seemed to stretch out to be almost half the size of the city above. Small warrens connected to larger warrens. Underground roads made of discarded brick and stone from above, homes and lean-to style buildings built from corrugated metal, wattle-and-daub, and wood, and small hand-drawn carts filled the smaller warrens. The larger warrens were where the homes seemed to be arranged, as well as "outdoor" markets.

The market she took me to had no sense or reason to it. Most of the items there were illegal, broken, or most likely stolen. "Is this some sort of black market or something?" I asked Nesta quietly.

She shook her head.

"A relief organization trying to help people?" I suggested, knowing I was wrong, but hoping that it was.

She shook her head again as her shoulders shook in controlled laughter. "No. This has been around since long before the Xathi. They've been around for much longer than I've been alive," she added.

"So, this has been under Duvest for a long time?" I asked as we sidestepped an overturned cart and headed towards a dark corner of the 'market'.

"As long as I can remember. Some people back home say that this place is older," she said.

"Do you believe that?"

She shrugged and pulled me around a corner and down another small street. At the end of the street were several buildings that stood at least three levels in height, and each building was home to a different herbalist shop on the ground floor. I counted five shops in total.

"What is this place?" I asked.

"Where we go for answers," Nesta said cryptically. She led me to the most run-down looking of the five shops, knocked six times on the door, then entered, pulling me in with her. The interior of the shop was filled with numerous shelves filled with herbs, plants, and powders of various colors. Many more hung from the ceiling, giving the shop an almost outdoor quality to it.

The scents that wafted around the interior of the shop were a mixture of something sweet, something mint, something citrus, and something almost rotting. I recognized some of the plants that were inside. I didn't know what their names were, but I had seen them before.

"My darling Nesta," came an elderly voice from a dark and smoky corner of the shop. A small woman that was nearly as round as she was tall, and she was not tall, waddled from behind a counter and approached Nesta, her arms opened wide. Her gray hair seemed to be pasted onto her head, while her wrinkles made her facial features difficult to make out clearly.

Nesta, with a massive smile on her face and genuine joy in her voice, greeted the woman with a big hug. "Gamma Prym." The two women hugged and spoke in quiet tones as I stood, waiting uncomfortably, near the entrance. As I waited and perused the shop, the women talked, occasionally gesturing towards me and sharing smiles.

There was an almost familial aspect to their relationship despite the fact that they looked nothing alike. I wondered at their relationship. Were they, in fact, related? Was Ms. Prym her grandmother, as Nesta had called her, or was that just a moniker used by everyone to refer to the little old woman?

Eventually, after I had gone up and down each of the shop's four aisles several times, Nesta called me over. "Sylor, this is Gamma Prym. Gamma Prym, this is Sylor. He's what's known as a Valorni," she said during her introduction.

I felt a bit uncomfortable as Gamma Prym looked me up and down. It felt a bit like an interrogator sizing up someone that they were getting ready to question. I felt thoroughly violated and frisked by the time she was done looking me over. "You're one of those aliens that came falling from the sky, aren't you?"

I nodded. "That is affirmative."

"Hm." She didn't seem impressed. She turned back to Nesta and patted her on the arm as she went back behind her counter. A moment later, her little head popped up from behind the counter as she settled herself on what I assumed to be a stool. "What did you need, my dear?"

"Well, you remember the weird attack that happened on the other side of Duvest a little while ago?" Nesta started, using the information I had given her as we had walked here.

"That I do, dearie," Gamma Prym said with a nod. "What about it?"

"Well, according to Sylor, the thing that attacked and created all of those holes in the surface is a massive plant-like creature and it's built a huge dome over Nyheim using those vines," Nesta explained.

"Mm-hmm, mm-hmm," our tiny shopkeeper said.

"Well," Nesta continued. "There's a toxin that Sylor and his people need, and they don't have enough back in Nyheim."

"And you were wondering if you could get some here," Gamma finished.

"Yes, ma'am," I said. She looked at me in mock surprise, almost as if she had forgotten that I was even there. She cocked her head to the side and studied me, again.

"Tell me, Sylor the Valorni," she said as her voice got low. "What is this creature and toxin that my darling Nesta is telling me about?"

"A giant sentient plant using its vines and shoots is threatening Nyheim. We believe the only thing that can stop it is either Narrissi extract, a variation, or something similar. Unfortunately, our scientists have only a small sample. They don't have enough to synthesize more."

"I see. And now you need this," she looked at Nesta for a moment, "Narrissi extract, you called it?"

"That's right, Gamma."

Prym nodded knowingly. "This toxin has many names. And it has underlying properties that I know you're looking for. It's not exactly a toxin, it's actually a secretion from a living thing. The problem is, though, we don't have any here."

"Where can we get some?" I asked.

"That's going to be the problem," Prym said with a deep sigh. "No one has gone to harvest any since you and the bugs first crashed here. So, you won't be able to get any from here."

I nodded in understanding. What that meant was that we would have to go to the source and harvest some for ourselves, and since it was a secretion from some sort of living creature, the hope was that it would be something small and non-dangerous. These people had harvested it in the past, so whatever creature they would get it from had to be at least semi-tame.

"Very well," I said in response. "Where do *we* go to get this secretion?"

"Well," Prym answered slowly. "I want you to understand something. No one has gone to harvest the secretion since your arrival because of the attack. Most of our equipment was destroyed and we're barely coming back to any sense of normality. However, even if we did have our equipment, there were only a few souls brave enough to venture into the home of the creature and get what you seek."

"The creature is dangerous, then?" I asked.

She nodded. "It is."

Regardless, I knew that we needed it and I was determined to go for it no matter the danger. If necessary, I would leave Nesta here with Prym while I traveled to wherever it was that I must go.

"Very well, I understand," I responded. "However, the toxin is needed. I fear that without it, soon the entire city of Nyheim will be crushed when this creature decides to end its search and decides we are no longer worth leaving alive."

With a heavy sigh, Gamma Prym nodded and looked to Nesta. "You are looking for a forest creature that lives within the Old Caverns. It is his teeth that hold the toxin. You must retrieve the teeth before they dry up and turn into dust."

Nesta's eyes went wide as she gasped. She knew what the creature was, while I remained in the dark. "No," she gasped once again.

"I'm sorry, dearie," Prym said gravely. "But it is the Kouldarc that you seek."

"What is a Kouldarc?" I asked.

"The Kouldarc is an old creature, older than most of us know," Prym answered me while she continued to look at Nesta. "It is dangerous, deadly to those not fast enough or strong enough. The Kouldarc lives in the Old Caverns, hunts at night, and rarely sees the day."

"What sort of equipment is used normally?" I inquired. I glanced at Nesta to see that she was still in shock to discover what the creature was.

Prym snorted. "Weapons, and a small machine meant to extract the secretion."

"And are there any more of these machines?" I asked.

She shook her head in the negative. "No. They were stored in a section of our warrens that the bugs found. There is nothing left."

I nodded in understanding. "Very well. Weapons I have," I said. "The rest, I'll figure out when the time comes."

Nesta looked at me in wonder. I winked at her and gave her a reassuring smile. I still did not know what a Kouldarc was. Prym's description was extremely vague, but we needed the toxin. I would just have to make sure that I was better and faster that whatever this creature was.

NESTA

"Which way?" Sylor asked me the moment we stepped out of Gamma Prym's shop. He had both hands on his hips, and he scanned the different streets in front of him with an attentive gaze. He was itching to make his way toward the Old Caverns, I could tell. I wondered if the idea of having to battle a blood-crazed Kouldarc was the reason behind his excitement. Even though Sylor seemed more cerebral than the other Valorni, the lust for battle still seemed to be a big part of him.

"Not so fast, big guy," I replied. "It's nighttime. We'll have to wait for the morning."

"Why?" he asked. "Isn't it all the same down here?"

"Well, it is," I explained. "But it's different when it

comes to the Old Caverns. No one goes there, especially not during the night. It's bad luck."

"Bad...luck?" He repeated me after, his smile made of equal parts amusement and confusion. The concept of superstition seemed to be a foreign one to him.

"Yeah," I nodded patiently. "See, there's more than just rock in those caverns. It used to house an old underground city. The first generation of black-market sellers that ventured under the ground in Duvest settled there, and they turned the place into a city. A mix of stone and tent. It's deserted now, though."

"Deserted? Why?"

"There was a massacre," I said, lowering my voice. The people in here didn't like to talk about that in the open, even if those things had happened more than a few generations ago. "Two factions of sellers were competing for control of the city, and they decided to make a deal. They met during the night in the main plaza, but both leaders were planning to use the meeting as a trap...suffice to say, the whole thing turned into a bloodbath fast. The battle lasted for days, or so the story goes, and a lot of innocent people died. The survivors settled here, in this place we're in."

"Do people think there are still soldiers down there?" he asked me, completely confused by my explanation. "If that happened so long ago, I doubt there's anyone there."

"Everyone knows that," I sighed. "It's just...people don't like it, alright? A lot of blood was shed there during the night, so people can't help but associate one thing with the other."

"I see," he said, but I could tell he still didn't understand the meaning of 'bad luck'. Apparently, the only thing the Valorni considered to be bad luck would be a depowered blaster rifle or a malfunctioning grenade. "So what do we do now?"

"We wait," I said with a smile. Truth be told, I was actually looking forward to spending some time just milling around the marketplace. I had visited the underground Duvest marketplace a lot when I was just a kid, curious about all the things littering all the different shop displays, and this whole trip had left me feeling a bit nostalgic.

"Wait where, exactly?"

"Come with me," I said, grabbing his hand and pulling him after me. We made our way through the tiny little streets, a few people glancing at Sylor as we went, and I happily noticed that everyone looked more curious than afraid. It seemed that the sentry's concerns were unfounded: nobody in here was freaking out because a massive green alien was walking among the crowd. If anything, they were fascinated by Sylor.

At the edge of the market, I immediately noticed a few stalls set up in front of what looked like a sea of tents. Some were so tiny that I doubted Sylor would fit inside them, but others looked massive enough to hold a small banquet. There were less tents in there than I remembered, but I supposed that was only normal. This was the underground's idea of a hotel and, since Duvest had turned into a ghost city, I guessed there weren't many travelers passing through here anymore.

"You have money, right?" I asked Sylor.

"I have enough back pay that I haven't been able to spend."

"Good, we're going to need it," I said. "Wait here, I'm going to get us a tent."

I went straight toward a man in one of the stalls and, just a few minutes later, I had negotiated a discount on one of the larger tents. I was pretty sure Sylor wouldn't appreciate me squandering his money on luxury accommodations, but he had no concept of the price of things down here. Besides, I had poured my heart and soul into getting us here: I had earned a reward.

"This is us," I told Sylor, pushing the front flaps of our tent to the side. A tall pole stood at the center of it, holding it all up, and what looked like a hundred pillows of different sizes had been laid out on the floor. "Oh, yes," I cried out, falling back on top of a mountain of pillows.

"This is…"

"Awesome?"

"Weird," Sylor said, tentatively sitting on top of some pillows. He looked uncomfortable. "Is this how everyone sleeps down here?"

"Not everyone," I laughed. "Just the lucky ones." Jumping to my feet, I went to the table that had been set in one of the corners and poured myself a glass of fresh water from the pitcher. There was also a bowl with grapes and some fresh peaches—not exactly a feast but, when it came to the underground, this was real luxury.

"Is that dinner?" Sylor asked, looking over my shoulder at the bowl of fruit on the table.

"No," I laughed, and then turned around and opened my hand. "Can I have some more of your money?" Frowning, he didn't argue with me. He had done a good job adjusting to human customs, but the underground lifestyle was in a completely different ballpark. He was like a fish out of water here, completely dependent on me.

I liked that, especially because I could manage all the money he had brought with him. Supposedly, these funds were meant to be used exclusively in the pursuit of our objective, but it wasn't like any of the sellers down there were handing out invoices. As far as I was concerned, I had a license to spend.

And that was exactly what I was going to do.

With Sylor's help, I started making the rounds. I visited each and every one of the food merchants stationed outside the traveler's precinct, and it didn't take long before we had a huge number of trays inside our tent. Laid out on a low table I had asked for, the food seemed to be calling out my name. From fried vegetables to grilled meat, we had a little of everything. I had even bought two pitchers of real beer, not the kind of watered-down piss that passed for alcohol these days in Nyheim.

"No food shortage in this place," Sylor said the moment we had finished our shopping spree. He stood at the end of the table, arms folded over his chest as he examined all the food we had bought. "How the skrell is there so much food in here?"

"Nyheim has been cut off from the other cities," I said. "Farmers can't get inside the city anymore, not while those vines are still there, but they need to get rid of their produce before it turns bad. If I had to guess, I'd say some of the Duvest merchants are already hanging out someplace between Nyheim and Duvest, and they're buying food they can sell down here at a discounted rate."

It was just a guess but, going from all the experience I had amassed living in the underground, I was pretty confident that my explanation was an accurate one. Of course, I didn't tell Sylor I had spent more than what a family of four would spend in a week. That information I kept to myself. If we were back in Nyheim, I'd feel guilty...but no one seemed to be going hungry in Duvest's underground.

"Are you going to just stare at the food?" I asked Sylor. I was already sitting at the table with my legs crossed, a large plate of boiled rice and beef in front of me. Just the smell of it was enough to make me feel alive. We had been surviving on military rations during our trip here, and eating real food for a change felt more than amazing.

"It does look good," Sylor finally said, and it didn't take long before he was trying a little of everything. He ate four times more than I did, and he emptied the two pitchers of beer by himself. By the time we were done, it seemed as if a famished mob had been eating with us.

"This felt good," Sylor laughed, one hand draped over his stomach. He threw himself back on top of the pillows, a satisfied look on his face. Back in Nyheim, he had probably been surviving on rations, eating far less than what he really wanted or needed. Now, though, he had made up for it.

Happy—nothing made me happier than a full stomach—I got up and joined Sylor, lying beside him on the bed we had improvised with the pillows and blankets. As I closed my eyes, I was almost surprised I wasn't thinking of anything. I didn't think of the Xathi, of the Nyheim vines, or Odeon's death.

I simply closed my eyes and fell asleep.

SYLOR

I had always been a light sleeper, so whenever Nesta moved in our small tent, I was aware of it. If tonight was any indication of how she slept, it was a wonder that she ever felt rested.

However, it wasn't her constant tossing and turning that had me uncomfortable. It was the small something that was poking me in the back. No matter where I moved, it seemed to be poking me right in the spine, and I couldn't reach it no matter how I stretched and contorted my arms.

Not wanting to wake Nesta, I quietly slipped out of the tent and stretched myself to my full height. I nodded politely to one of the local denizens, who returned my nod, and I motioned for him to come near. "I do not mean to bother you," I whispered. "But there is something in the middle of my back that I cannot reach. Would you be so kind?"

He nodded with a slight smile. I turned around and before I could speak, he grunted in surprise. He put one hand on my back, then grabbed whatever was poking me and pulled. I felt something tug at my skin, then heard a small slurping noise as whatever was attached to my back was finally removed.

My new friend showed me what he had removed. It was some sort of small, slimy creature with a suction-cup mouth, black in color and shiny in the underground light that shined down from above. My quizzical look expressed the question on my mind, and he answered quietly. "It's a leech. We sometimes have them down here, especially when it rains up above. They are harmless, but annoying, little bloodsuckers."

He dropped it on the ground then stepped on it, a loud squishing noise accompanied with a short squeal. I honestly felt a little sorry for the creature. "If they are harmless, why did you kill it?"

He shrugged. "They bother me. Good night," he finished with a smile and walked away.

Absentmindedly scratching near the spot where the leech had attached itself, I shook my head in wonder and quietly went back into the tent. I readjusted my sleeping area and crawled back in under the sheet. As I moved to get comfortable, Nesta rolled over and curled up against me. I attempted to move so she could be comfortable, but as I moved, her arm snaked up and over me. She lightly nuzzled me and made a sound that almost sounded like a light "coo."

I smiled. I actually liked how she felt against me. Her lithe little body, with her surprisingly soft skin, felt nice, almost comfortable. Her body heat mingled with mine, making the coolness of the warren bearable.

I looked down at her. Her projected toughness was gone, replaced by innocence. Her protective walls were down, and she finally seemed to be at peace with herself and her life. Perhaps sleep was the only time she allowed herself to be off her guard. I gently moved my arm out from under her and wrapped it around her. I put my left hand under my head and closed my eyes.

I woke up later to see Nesta staring up at me.

"Hi," she said sweetly.

"Hi," I breathed out. "Sleep well?"

"Mmm. Guess you're pretty comfortable to sleep on," she joked, a little grin on her face as she spoke.

"Well, I've always been told that I have soft skin," I joked. It was true, my father used to say that I was soft-skinned whenever I showed any form of compassion towards something.

Luckily, Nesta didn't catch the hidden meaning. "Mm, yeah, you do," she said, running her fingers lightly up my chest. She traced little lines on my chest, a light smile gracing her lips as she touched me. It felt good to feel those fingers on me. Her touch was so light and gentle that I felt little bumps form on my skin.

"That feels good," I said, gruffly.

"I like it, too."

Her fingers continued to stroke me lazily.

"Your fingers are powerful, for someone so small."

"I can bring a giant beast like you to heel."

"And I can make you moan."

She giggled lightly. "I gave you goosebumps with my fingers. I wonder what I'll give you with this." She crawled her way up and leaned in close to me. I brought my face up to hers and kissed her. My lips touched hers and we grabbed onto one another, forcing our lips harder against one another. Her tongue was the first to part lips and I enjoyed the sweet saltiness that accompanied her tongue.

Suddenly, Nesta pulled away from me, a look of confusion on her face. "What is it?" I asked.

"We...we," she stuttered a bit as she found her words. "We just kissed, but we don't like one another. Do we?"

"Don't we?" I asked. She blushed and tried to bury her face in my chest. It was adorable. "I don't think I've ever seen you blush like this," I said as I ran my hand through her hair.

"And I'm pretty sure you've never had goosebumps before," she shot back playfully.

She pulled herself up from me and brought her hands down, rubbing me as she began to open my pants. She took my cock out and let out a small gasp as it was finally freed. She then grabbed me again and began to stroke me, bringing an almost animalistic growl of pleasure from me. I felt the wetness of her lips cover me and I couldn't take it anymore. I grabbed her head and began to thrust myself into her mouth.

"Skrell," I moaned as she continued her ministrations.

The sound of sucking and moaning began to fill the air of our tent.

With one last thrust, I came hard in her mouth.

She continued to suck my cock until I was spent.

We lay there for a long moment, collecting our breath.

"Unfortunately," she said with a groan as she pulled herself away from me, "we need to go."

I hated that she pulled away from me, but she was correct. We needed the toxin and there wasn't time for personal enjoyment, not yet. I nodded as I sat up. "You're right, but soon..." We quickly got dressed, gathered our gear, and left the tent. I made a show of holding the tent flap open for Nesta. She lightly ran her hand across my chest and smiled up at me as she walked past.

We walked together away from where we had spent the night towards the rear of the market. At the far the end of the warren, where the remnants of the vendors' wares and booths stood, was a tunnel. While I didn't think much of the tunnel itself, I did happen to notice that the mouth of the tunnel was clear. The other tunnels had either a small guard station or supplies piled up near them, but this one was empty. There was nothing within five to ten yards of this one.

"I guess this is the tunnel then," I remarked.

"Uh-huh." She did not look happy, but I could see in her eyes that she was resolute and determined to proceed. "This is how we get to the Old Caverns. Should take us a couple of hours to get there."

"Ah, a short jaunt. I approve," I said, attempting to put a bit of humor into my tone.

"Ha," she responded. We began our trek into the tunnel. It was wide, nearly twelve feet across and about ten feet tall. I had to jump to reach the ceiling.

"Do you know what created this tunnel?" I asked as a way of making conversation.

Nesta shook her head. "No. This one is older than us, here long before the city grew underground."

"I see." We continued on for a while in silence before I decided to try conversing again. "How do you know so much about things down here? You look very young, almost too young to know so much."

She cleared her throat before answering. "Well, thank you for the compliment, I think. I'm nineteen and I grew up down here. Well, not here, specifically," she amended. "But, you know what I mean."

I nodded to show that I did.

She took a deep breath and continued on. "I...I don't really know who my parents were. I grew up as a ward to one of the bigger dealers. He ran the market back under Nyheim. When I was younger, he used to bring me here whenever he had a delivery to make or something to pick up. He taught me everything I know."

Her voice was humble and reserved as she spoke. It made me feel respect for this man. Then, something made me wonder. "You speak about him in the past tense," I stated.

She nodded. "Yes, I did. I..." she sighed, and her head dropped a fraction of an inch. "I don't think he's alive anymore. I haven't been able to find him since the Xathi attack."

"I'm sorry," I said as I placed my hand on her shoulder. She reached up and patted my hand, giving me a sad smile.

Then her expression changed as she looked up at

me. "Wait a minute. How old are you? I told you my age, without really meaning to, so you tell me yours."

"Well," I said as I thought about it. "While a standard year here is not the same as a year on my homeworld, I believe that it is close enough to not make a significant difference."

"What do you mean?" she asked.

I tilted my head to the side as I smiled at her. "Well, based on what I've learned of this world since we've been here, your people chose this planet because it was within certain parameters of the human homeworld of Earth. An Earth year is three-hundred and sixty-five days long. A year here is three-hundred and fifty days long. A year on my world is three-hundred and seventy-three days long."

"Wow," she interjected, a bit surprised if I read her facial expression correctly.

I nodded. "As I said, not much difference. Based on Valorni calendars, I have seen twenty-eight years pass since my birth. As a matter of fact," I added, "the commemoration of my birth is soon upcoming. Approximately two months away."

"So, your birthday is only two months away. That means that your birthday is in our winter season," she said after doing some counting in her head.

"It would seem so, although on my homeworld, I was born in the late spring," I explained.

"Wow. Maybe, one day, you could take me there," she said as we walked around a bend in the tunnel.

"Perhaps," I said. She was young, had grown up without parents, and was a survivor. She had been used as a thief for much of her life. She knew nothing else. It had to be that way, it was the only scenario that made sense. I wanted to question her about it when I noticed that she was staring intently ahead. I looked forward... we had arrived.

NESTA

"The Old Caverns," I muttered, my heart tightening into a scared little fist. Our flashlight illuminated the cavernous place in front of us, stalactites hanging from the ceiling like daggers, projecting their elongated shadows across the walls. "Quiet now," I warned Sylor, and we carefully made our way inside the cavern.

I put one foot after the other cautiously, trying not to make a sound, but my heart was beating so loudly I couldn't stop myself from being afraid whatever dwelled here in the depths would hear me.

There was no sign of the tents that once had formed the old city, their canvas and poles long gone, and only ripped pieces of fabric that had been discarded lay on the ground. They were so old that they disintegrated easily, the sole of my boots destroying them as I pressed them against the earth.

"Look," I whispered, pointing the flashlight toward the walls. Old etchings of faces, buildings, and flowers covered their surface, telling a story of the first people that had come here from the surface. There were also drawings of a creature as dark as the night, its eyes burning with murderous intent. Just that drawing was enough to make my throat go dry.

Few dared go after a Kouldarc, and I still remembered all the stories Odeon used to tell me about the men that went on a hunt, never to return. The creature thrived in the shadows, the silence of the depths its only companion, and only a few brave but suicidal hunters dared go after it...and that with all manners of equipment. The fact that I only had a flashlight in my hand did nothing to help my nerves. Sure, I had Sylor, but still...

"Don't be nervous," he told me in a whisper, his hand on my shoulder. I didn't say anything to him, but I laid my hand on top of his. His fingers squeezed my shoulder kindly, and I felt myself growing more relaxed. Even though we were so different, he seemed to know exactly what I was feeling.

"This isn't going to be easy," I said after a few minutes of walking. "The Kouldarc only moves in the shadows. It blends in with the darkness, where it feels safe, so I think our flashlight won't help."

"I might have a solution for that," he said promptly, grabbing his backpack and laying it on the ground. He knelt before it and, while I held the flashlight, he started unpacking. He unfolded a roll of canvas on the floor, then grabbed a few electronics from a small metallic case.

"What are you doing?"

"You'll see," he said, momentarily looking up at me.

Grabbing a datapad he carried with him, he popped out the case back with the tip of his knife and start untangling a few wires. Before I knew it, he had hooked up a few electronics to the datapad. Using a pair of braces, he then secured the datapad to his backpack.

"Hold this," he said as he removed the scope of his laser rifle, handing it to me. He then tapped the datapad a few times, and two seconds later the scope in my hands lit up. "Try it."

Having no idea what I'd see, I held the scope up and pressed it against my right eye. To my surprise, I could now see into the darkness, a green glow covering the surface of the walls and the floor.

"Those scope models are old, and don't have night vision," he explained, "but I managed to hook it up to a program I just coded in the datapad. Now the scope is feeding the visuals straight into the datapad, which converts the signals into something we can actually see, and then it feeds that signal back to the lenses."

"You did this *now?*" I asked him, momentarily forgetting where I was and raising my voice. I had met a lot of men that knew their way around electronics, but I had never seen anyone work so fast and with so little warning. No wonder the Valorni had pegged Sylor as their weapons designer: he was more than just talented...he was gifted. "That's...that's amazing, Sylor."

"Thank you, Nesta," he returned, a proud smile spreading on his lips. It seemed there was no easier way to make Sylor smile than to compliment him on his handiwork. He really prided himself on his creations.

"So... I guess I have to turn this off now?" I asked him, hesitantly looking down at the flashlight in my hands. Even though I knew that walking in the darkness was the best shot we had at finding a Kouldarc, I didn't like the idea one bit. As fun as it was to hunt some murderous creature inside an abandoned city that had been the place of a massacre, it was hard not to prefer being back at the tent, where I could enjoy a nice breakfast without having an ancient creature trying to murder me.

"Yes, turn it off," Sylor nodded, still looking as relaxed as always. He was either underestimating the strength of a Kouldarc, or he simply wasn't afraid of it.

Being that Sylor was the kind of guy that calculated every move of his, my bet was on the latter.

And if Sylor wasn't afraid, then I'd just follow his lead.

Taking a deep breath, I turned the flashlight off. The darkness swallowed us whole in a heartbeat and, for a moment, panic started taking over my mind. As if he had been anticipating it, Sylor just reached for me and held my hand. Grabbing his improvised scope with his other hand, he held it up as he started marching deeper into the cavern.

Our pace slowed down considerably, since Sylor was now the only one of us that could see, but he guided me carefully through the uneven ground of the cavern. His hand remained on mine, his large fingers making mine feel so delicate that I almost felt like a child again.

We spent the next two hours simply walking further into the caverns, but always avoiding the tunnels that ventured deeper than I felt comfortable with. Still, there was no sign of any Kouldarc.

"I think we have to go deeper," I whispered, holding Sylor's hand more tightly. I didn't like the idea of entering the tunnels this deep underground, but it seemed as if we had no choice. We couldn't return to Nyheim without the toxin. Sylor would never accept defeat and, somehow, I had bought into his crusade. If the people of Nyheim needed me to do this, then I would do it.

"Deeper, yes," Sylor whispered back at me, already leading the way there. "Don't be afraid, Nesta. I'll die before I let anything happen to you. You're safe with me."

"Thank you," I found myself saying, pressing my body against his. Because I knew he wouldn't be able to see me in the dark, I let a smile spread across my lips. I had no idea what the hell Sylor had done to me, but I really felt safe around him. More than just safe, I felt comfortable.

For a long time, I had never let anyone come close. The members of my old gang were the only ones I let in, and I'd just keep my distance from anyone else. Trust didn't come easy for me, but it was different with Sylor. And it was more than just trust or comfort...somehow, I was starting to really like him.

"Stop," he suddenly whispered, freezing in place. I had no idea why he had stopped, but I just did what he told me and didn't say a word.

Then, I heard it.

Coming from the depths, a growl.

The Kouldarc was close.

SYLOR

The growl echoed through the cavern. Instinctively, I reached out and grabbed Nesta, pulling her behind me. There was little to see with the scope as I slowly panned back and forth, searching for the creature.

Another growl came, the echo making it difficult to pinpoint its location. Nesta tapped me on the left elbow, directing my attention. I slowly panned to my left, and soon came across movement. I caught sight of a leg going behind a boulder, so I concentrated my attention on that boulder and waited. Soon, the creature moved from behind its cover and I was able to get my first good look at the Kouldarc. A quick glance in its direction without the scope showed me that the Kouldarc melded almost perfectly with the dark. When it blinked, its eyes flashed a bright yellow for a brief moment before fading back into the dark.

Using the scope once again, I was able to study it as it studied us. It had an almost feline quality to it, except for the six legs. Its long, lithe body moved fluidly, while its three whip-like tails waved back and forth like saplings in the wind. It opened its mouth and let out a noise that sounded like a whispered roar.

It must not have thought us a threat. As quickly as I could, I snapped the scope onto my blaster and brought it up. The Kouldarc had moved, it took me a brief moment to find it again. It was moving slowly, patiently, towards our right. I felt the hair on the back of my neck stand on end as it stepped towards us and I was able to see the Kouldarc's paws. Even ten yards away from it as we were, I could see that its paws were massive, about the size of my own hands, and the paws ended in six razor-sharp, three-inch claws that made no noise when they hit the cavern floor.

I took aim and it must have seen me, for its head tilted to the side in curiosity. Not wanting to squander the moment, I fired and watched as nothing happened. My blaster fire seemed to simply absorb into the creature. It let out a series of short hisses that sounded almost like laughter.

"Do you have any idea how to kill it?" I whispered back to Nesta, who had laid her head against my back. I could feel her head move side-to-side in a negative. "I thought not. Well, blasters don't work. I wonder what else we can try before he attacks us."

I returned to watching the Kouldarc as it moved and paced in front of us. It stayed back from us, almost as if it wasn't sure of us, either. Our staring contest continued for minutes before I became aware of something. Its coloration and movements seemed to make it part of the darkness, as if the darkness were another skin for it.

That was it! The darkness. I reached behind me and pulled Nesta forward. She resisted at first, but I was firm. "Hold this," I whispered sternly as I put the blaster in her hands. "Keep an eye on it…there," I said as I helped her find the creature.

As she maintained a visual on the creature, I reached into my side pack and pulled out a flare. I quickly took the flare apart and removed the wick. "Come with me," I said as I gently pulled Nesta back into the lighted part of the caverns. I had her hold the scope up for me to look through. The Kouldarc stayed where it was, sitting on its haunches, watching us.

I took the blaster back from Nesta and quickly removed two rounds. "Watch," I told her. I quickly attached the wick of the flare to one of the rounds, then added the blasting cap. What I had essentially done was create a modified flare-round. Since I did not have a flare gun, I was forced to improvise. "Now, do the same," I said to her as I handed her the other round and another flare.

I emptied the blaster of the regular rounds, inserted my modified flare, then waited for Nesta to finish the other one. I wanted her to do it because I wanted her to be able to care for herself if she were ever away from me and in a situation where improvisation was needed.

She finished the round, as I had done, and handed it to me with shaking hands. "Is it right?" she asked.

I nodded. "Perfect. You've got a knack for this." I quickly loaded the round, then loaded the remaining rounds back into the blaster. I clicked off the safety, brought the blaster up, and looked again for the Kouldarc. There it sat, watching me. It had not moved.

"Stay here," I cautioned. I walked back into the darkness, getting close enough to the creature that I could hear it breathing. It still sat, watching me, its three tails sweeping back and forth across the cavern floor. I took a deep breath and quickly came up with a plan.

As quickly as I could, I pointed the blaster in the air and fired. As the round flew up, I brought the barrel back down. The Kouldarc was moving, quickly. He cleared the distance between us in one and a half bounds of its six powerful legs. As it was in the air, I fell to the ground and averted my eyes to guard against the explosion of the flare. The cavern lit up brightly as the creature's screams filled my ears. It crashed to the ground beside me and I turned and fired the second round directly into its quivering torso.

The flare erupted and covered the beast in flames, its shrieks and screams both frightening and pitiful. I felt sorry for the beast, if only for a moment. I regained my feet and moved away as it twitched and writhed in pain.

Nesta rushed over and fairly tackled me back down to the ground. "I thought it had gotten you," she whispered desperately as we lay on the ground. Before I could answer, she plunged down and kissed me, her tongue nearly breaking through my teeth to reach my own. Her enthusiasm and passion overwhelmed me and I returned the fire.

I ran my hands up and down her back as she kissed me, my hands gently caressing the small of her back before I moved them down to her firm and amazing hind quarters. She moaned as I grabbed her and pushed herself against me, grinding against me, getting my blood rushing.

The pleasure that I felt was intense, but I was determined to make it last. I refused to let myself go, not without being able to feel all of her. As she pulled her head up to breathe, she smiled at me. Then she looked past me and nearly cursed.

"What is it?" I asked as I craned my neck to look. The creature was dissolving before our eyes.

"We still need to get the toxin," she said as she climbed off me. I hated to have her leave me, but she was correct. The toxin was of vital importance. As she rushed over to begin extracting the teeth, I straightened my pants and gained my feet. I reached into my pack that had fallen off when she tackled me and extracted the case we had brought with us.

She pulled carefully at the teeth, using a small pair of clamps that she had brought with her. If any of the teeth excreted the toxin while she pulled, the clamps would keep her protected. I kneeled next to her as she pulled one tooth, then another, placing them carefully in the case. She managed to extract five teeth before the Kouldarc turned to dust, taking the rest of its teeth with it.

She looked up at me, a sense of pride, fear, and desire on her face. "We did it," she breathed.

I nodded. I could scarcely contain my desire for her. The feel of her hands, her skin, and her lips against me kept my adrenaline pumping, kept my mind thinking about her and what her body would look like without clothes.

I smiled at her in hopes that my smile would rekindle our earlier actions. As I held my hand out to her, another growl filled the cavern, a much louder and deeper growl than before. Not wishing to discover the size of the creature that owned such a growl, I grabbed Nesta and we escaped the cavern, grabbing our packs as we went.

We headed away from the cavern and back into the tunnel, keeping an eye behind us. It wasn't very long before I was comfortable enough to slow down our pace and walk.

Her hand was small, painfully small, in my own, but it felt right. I wanted her, desired her, and wished to feel those hands against my body again. To feel her hands draw themselves slowly down my chest and across parts of me...I wished for that to be something that I could feel for the rest of my days.

NESTA

We made our way back to the marketplace in a state of pure euphoria, the toxin safely stored inside Sylor's backpack. The fight against the Kouldarc hadn't been an easy one, but Sylor hadn't flinched in the face of danger. On the contrary...he seemed to thrive whenever his life was on the line.

While most men would balk at the impossible task in front of them, Sylor hadn't even hesitated before rising up to meet the challenge. And all that even though he was doing it to protect a species that wasn't his own.

There was more to the Valorni than met the eye, apparently.

"Tired?" he asked me, the lights from the marketplace already glowing up ahead. I breathed out with relief as I started hearing the usual chatter from the vendors, and only when I considered Sylor's question did I realize every single muscle in my body seemed as heavy as lead. Even something as simple as keeping my eyes open was taking a massive amount of effort.

"I'm exhausted," I sighed, but even my exhaustion wasn't enough to wipe the smile off my face. The memories of Sylor's body were still fresh in my mind, and that ensured my smile would be etched on my face for hours to come.

"I know," he said softly. "So am I."

Gently laying his large hand on my lower back, his fingers brushing against the patch of bare skin between my shirt and pants, he looked into my eyes and smiled. I returned it, closing my eyes for a moment as I enjoyed the way I had my hand tucked inside his.

"Finally," Sylor groaned the moment we stepped inside our tent. Taking his backpack off, he placed it in one of the corners, hiding it under a series of pillows, and then almost collapsed on our improvised bed of blankets. I dragged my feet toward where he was and, like a deflated balloon, I crashed next to him.

"Thank you, Nesta," he breathed out as I turned to face him. Even though he was tired, his eyes were still full of life.

"For what?" I asked, closing the distance between

the two of us and laying my head on his chest. I closed my eyes as I heard the gentle beating of his heart, my fingers tracing the contour of his toned pectorals.

"For everything," he replied, his voice nothing but a whisper. "You might have saved Nyheim."

"I only came this far because of you," I said, not even bothering with lying. "If it weren't for you..." I trailed off then, the exhaustion in my muscles slowly seeping into my mind. The rest of my sentence died in my throat, and I felt my consciousness drifting away from me. The only thing I still felt from the waking world were Sylor's fingers, woven in my hair as he gently caressed me.

I slept more peacefully than I had in years, and when my eyelids fluttered open, I was still in the same position. Slowly raising my head, I glanced at the tent's entrance and sighed with relief as I realized it was still nighttime, the dim lights of the underground's marketplace indicating the passage of time. I still had a few more hours of sleep ahead of me.

"Already awake?" I heard Sylor ask me, and I rolled to the side so that I was facing him. He was looking at me with lazy eyes, his mellow voice telling me he must've woken up while I was trying to see if it was morning already.

"No," I smiled, my words as soft as his. "I'm still dreaming," I continued, reaching for him and delicately brushing my thumb over his parted lips. His eyes never left mine as I did it, and I felt something in his gaze. Desire?

No...it was more than that.

It was hunger.

Scooting over so that my whole body was pressed against his, I took my fingers from his lips and then closed my eyes. Taking my time, I rested my forehead against his and then waited.

"Nesta..." Sylor whispered, laying one hand on my right hip. I felt his fingers sliding under my shirt, his fingertips caressing my naked skin, and that was when I felt his lips against mine. The moment I felt his tongue part my lips, I completely lost it. I surrendered to the same hunger that burned in Sylor's eyes, and I let desire take me over.

"I'm right here," I told him, rolling on top of his body so that I was straddling him. I felt his hardness straining against his pants, and I laid both my hands on his chest and threw my head back. Grinding against him, I moaned softly as I felt his rock-hard desire.

This time, I wouldn't let anything stop me.

This time, I would go all the way.

"I want you, Nesta," he said, his right hand resting on the curve of my ass. His fingers dug into my flesh, and another moan exploded from between my lips as he reached up with his free hand and started massaging my breast. I felt my nipples harden up, my shirt suddenly becoming uncomfortable, and I simply pulled it over my head. "I *need* you," Sylor continued, lowering his voice as his words fell into a tense growl.

"Then shut up and take me," I threw back at him, both my hands on his chest. Leaning down, I crushed my mouth against his and allowed our tongues to dance around one another, Sylor's hands busy with exploring every inch of my body. We kissed in a frenzy, the desire I felt quickly turning into an unstoppable tidal wave, and I just tore his shirt off his body.

I held my breath and, pulling my lips off his, I took a moment to appreciate his half-naked body. His muscles were so perfectly delineated that it seemed as if his body had been carved out of marble by a master sculptor's chisel, the purple bands that crawled up and down his arms somehow making him look even stronger than he already was.

Never allowing my eyes to leave his, I scooted down his legs slightly, my fingertips slowly making their way down his chest. I felt the grooves of his abs under my fingers, a shiver running up my spine as his muscles tensed under my touch, and I only stopped when I felt his hard member pulsing against the palm of my right hand.

I knew Sylor was a gifted Valorni but, oh, that word applied to so much more than just his talents with weaponry design. I had already had him between my lips, his warm flesh throbbing with desire against my tongue, but as I curled my fingers around his thickness...it somehow felt like the first time once more. I massaged him over his pants for a short moment, but it didn't take long before I was pulling his pants down his legs, freeing his erection.

"Your body," he demanded, rolling to the side and pinning me against the floor. "I want to see it." He didn't wait for a response. Instead, he just knelt between my legs and unlaced my pants. Leaning down, he sucked one nipple into his mouth as he pulled my pants down my legs, his tongue carefully circling my aching extremity.

"You're delicious," he continued, the tip of his tongue sliding down the curve of my breast. He kept going down, both lips and tongue traveling over my belly, and only stopped when he met the elastic band of my underwear. Holding it with his teeth, he then simply pulled as hard as he could, the sound of fabric ripping and tearing making me moan with anticipation.

"Don't make me wait," I begged him, propping myself up on both my elbows. Breathing hard, I reached for him and curled my fingers around his hardness, flicking my wrist as my fingers traveled up and down his length. I knew little about the Valorni, but it seemed that not only their muscles were impressive. Sylor was an impressive specimen, I had no doubts about it...in fact, I was surprised I could wrap my fingers around his hard member.

"Come here," he growled, hooking his fingers under the back of my knees. Dragging me across the pillows toward him, he closed the distance between both our bodies and then...

"I want you," I moaned as I felt him, hard and wild, against my wetness. Lacing my legs around his waist, I pulled him toward me with a kind of desperate urgency, and Sylor did exactly what I needed him to do.

One thrust and he was inside me.

My eyes rolled in their orbits as I felt his rock-hard member strain against my insides, each movement of his hips sending flames of violent delight up my spine. Digging my fingernails into his shoulder blades, I just surrendered to the moment and let him take me.

My body was his.

"So good," Sylor growled, his eyes on mine. "Nesta, you're...amazing."

"Only noticed now?" I teased him, but the last part of my sentence was drowned by a moan escaping from between my lips. Ecstasy lashed out of every single nerve ending I had, and even my mind seemed as if it were on fire.

Acting on pure instinct, I rolled, laying both hands on his chest and pushing him back, followed after him, never allowing him to leave my body, and started rocking my hips against his own the moment I had my knees on either side of his body.

I rode him as hard as I could, enjoying the way his hands desperately explored every curve there was on my body, from my ass to my breasts. I went as hard as I could, beads of sweat already appearing on my forehead, and I let a kind of wicked fury take over my movements.

"I'm gonna...I'm gonna...!" I started to say, but I didn't even get to finish my sentence. Before I knew what was happening, my heart had started drumming violently, my body tensing up like a nocked arrow. That tidal wave of pleasure finally crashed against my body and, for a moment, I thought that my consciousness had deserted me.

Sylor, though, brought me back to reality.

Thrusting upward, both his hands firmly planted on my hips, he kept on unleashing pleasure all over my body. Each thrust of his felt like heaven and, the moment his cock became even harder than before, his whole body tensing up like mine had done just moments before, I readied myself for what was about to happen.

"SYLOR!" I screamed out, another orgasm spreading its wings deep inside me. My muscles twitched, my breath grew ragged, and it seemed my brain was working overtime to keep me conscious. Each time Sylor's cock throbbed against my inner walls, delivering his seed into my body, a quivering moan tumbled from my mouth.

"Nesta," he whispered quietly, the electric frenzy that had taken over both our bodies slowly fading. Reaching up, he delicately pushed a lock of hair away from my face. "Are you alright?"

Smiling, I rolled to the side and collapsed on top of the pillows, next to Sylor's naked body. His question was a silly one. After all, there was only one possible answer.

"I've never been better."

SYLOR

I awoke to Nesta's naked form cradled against my own. I ran my fingers lightly down her arm as her head rested against my chest. She let out a mild moan and shifted a bit, a smile across her face as she remained asleep.

I thought back to last night, to how our time with one another fed my emotions like no other action in my life. To have been inside her, to feel her move against me and grind her body against mine, I wanted that feeling again. I shifted slightly and brought my free hand up to caress her shoulder lightly, slowly bringing my hand down to her breast.

"Are you really wanting more?" she whispered with her eyes still closed.

"Do you blame me?" I whispered back. "Last night

was a feeling that I wish to repeat as often as we can."

She chuckled lightly and started to run her hand down my chest, to my waist, finally resting upon my cock. "Hmm," she started. "Looks like you might be ready to go again."

"And you?" I asked.

"Of course," she smiled. Then, an unusual noise emanated within the tent. She looked up at me and began to laugh. I joined her. My own stomach joined hers in rumbling and our laughter grew. "Maybe we should eat something first," she suggested.

"I agree." We untangled ourselves from one another and put our clothes on. Within minutes, we were exiting the tent. "Where should we go?" I asked.

She shrugged, then smiled. "I know somewhere you might like." She led me to a small stall where a middle-aged man stood over several pots and pans. The smell wafting from his stall made my mouth water. "John," she said happily as we approached the stall.

He looked at the both of us in confusion for a moment, then settled on Nesta. She sidled up to the stall, her prettiest smile on display. Finally, recognition hit him and he let out a loud bark of laughter. His booming voice echoed as he answered her. "Nesta!" As he came out from behind the stall, he walked with a heavy limp and I quickly discovered why…his left foot was gone, replaced by a poorly fitting prosthetic.

"Where have you been, darling?" he asked as he scooped her up in a massive hug that seemed to swallow her. He was as tall as I was, heftier than I, and you could see the power that he must have once had. I wondered what his profession had been before he ended up down here.

"Can't. Breathe," Nesta joked as he hugged her. He set her down and held her by her shoulders, looking her up and down. She looked up into his eyes. "I've been trying to make it day-to-day, my friend. At the moment, I'm starving."

"Ha! Of course, of course," he boomed as he let her go and went back behind his stall. "Why else would you come to visit old John?"

"You know better than that," Nesta said as she sat at one of the stools in front of his stall, indicating that I should take the other. "I love seeing you."

He winked at her as he scoffed, then sneezed into his elbow. "You always were able to make old John feel better. Now, what can I be getting you and your green friend?" His looks in my direction were filled with actual kindness, as well as a bit of protective zeal.

I nodded to him and he returned my nod.

"What have you got today?" Nesta asked.

"Well, on this morning's menu are some Corven eggs, a bit of Binseg stew, and some fresh bread, courtesy of Ms. Jamis," he said as he tapped each pan or pot in succession.

"That old woman is still kicking?" Nesta asked through a barely held back chuckle.

"Aye," John nodded as he grabbed some plates. "And she'll probably be kicking long after we're both dead."

"Too damn stubborn to die," Nesta joked. They both laughed as I sat there, absorbing the moment. I had no desire to interrupt and force my way into their enjoyment. "Well, John, we'll take each and keep it coming."

"You always did have a strong appetite. Enjoy," John said as he filled our plates and set them before us. As we ate, Nesta introduced me to John and we held a pleasant conversation. I learned that John used to be a soldier until an accident took his foot. When he lost his family and a chance at work, he fell into a bad time until he discovered life down here. He was happy, and that's all he wanted.

After we ate, Nesta and I returned to our tent to gather our gear. "Want to look around a little?" Nesta asked.

I shrugged. "Why not." I knew that we must return, but a short time looking around wouldn't hurt. Perhaps we would be able to find something down here that I could use.

Nesta led me back to the market and we spent our time browsing. In several of the booths, Nesta seemed to be reuniting with people she knew from her youth. In others, I found a few things, parts and components, that I felt I would be able to use. I purchased them, overpaying a bit in order to help. Each vendor thanked me and Nesta gave me a small pat on my arm or a hug each time.

We were well into the middle of the market when Nesta suddenly stopped walking. She stood stiff, her eyes wide. I was unable to tell if she was angry or shocked. Her skin paled as she looked across the market. I looked as well, but could not see what could possibly have gotten her attention in such a way.

"Nesta?"

She ignored me and began walking through the crowd, weaving her way through them with ease. I tried to follow, but my size slowed me down. As I tried to gently push my way through, I kept my eye on Nesta. She was approaching an older looking gentleman, older than John. He had noticed her as well and was making his own way towards her.

He opened his arms and put a smile on his face. I wasn't close enough to hear what was said, but I could tell Nesta was angry. She pushed the older man, and was yelling at him.

I missed most of what she was saying, but I finally managed to get close enough to hear "...you bastard! How could you do that to me?"

I reached out and caught her before she could push him again. "What's the matter?" I asked.

She looked back at me and calmed slightly. "This?" she asked, pointing at the man. "This is the man that raised me."

I was shocked. She had told me that he was dead.

She must have seen the look on my face. "I thought he was dead, too. This is Odeon, leader of Sabre, my mentor, and the man that 'died' during the Xathi attack."

I looked at the man. He was not a big man, thin, but not sickly. He must have been in his sixties, if you could trust the wrinkles on his face and hands. His arms were covered in tattoos and his nearly bald head was covered in stubble, as if he had shaved his head only a few days before and had yet to do so again.

I had an instant dislike for the man. The way he looked at Nesta, and how his eyes rarely left her, made my hands itch for a weapon. I remained calm as he looked at her, a profound sense of disappointment on his face.

"Nesta," his falsetto voice carrying a little too much innocence. "You wrong me, my dear."

"Wrong you?" Nesta nearly shouted. "You were supposed to be dead. You left me alone, to fend for myself, and you left the group to falter and break apart. You abandoned us!"

"Please, let me…"

"Explain?" she shouted. "Explain what?"

He looked at me, a look that seemed to ask me for assistance. Not wishing to oblige him, but wanting Nesta to calm down, I pulled her aside. "You need to calm down," I said gently, regretting my words instantly.

The anger flashed in her eyes as she looked at me.

"I…I did not mean for my words to come out that way," I quickly explained. "I am merely trying to keep you from losing your temper. Perhaps he has a reason."

"A reason for abandoning me?" she growled.

I nodded, slowly. "I do not condone his actions, or defend them. I am merely stating that you should allow him the opportunity to speak, to discover what he has done and why." I looked back at him and resisted the urge to break his face. The smile on his face made me want to vomit. I turned my attention back to Nesta. "And if you don't accept his words then, you can beat him half to death for all I care."

She looked at me and grinned. It was an almost feral grin, but at least her anger was sated, at least a little bit.

I turned back around and let Nesta go. She carefully, slowly, and methodically stepped towards him. His smile grew as she approached and her anger returned. I was unable to blame her, I wanted to see what it felt like to have his jaw break beneath my fists.

NESTA

"Why don't you come join me for tea?" Odeon asked us. I really wasn't in the mood for tea, I was in the mood to boot him halfway across the warren and back.

So I was surprised when I agreed to sit and have tea with him. I grabbed Sylor and dragged him along with me as I followed the man that raised me through the market to a small building that looked like it had been carved out of the cave.

"Come in, come in," Odeon said with a flourish as he pulled aside the curtain that was acting as the door. "Please don't mind the mess, I've been struggling to find a reliable maid to help me keep this place looking respectable."

We walked inside and I was blown away. 'Don't

mind the mess,' he said. Hah! What mess? This place was immaculate. If there was anything that could be called a mess within this first room, it would be that there was a glass still on the table that took up the middle of the room.

There were six chairs sitting around the rectangular table that looked to be made from solid wood. How he got a wood table down here was beyond me, but he seemed to be very proud of it. The interior of his stone home was adorned with artwork and the interior had been white-washed to bring light and brightness to it. On the wall opposite the entrance hung a piece of artwork that took up the entire wall.

To my left was the entrance to what looked like the kitchen, while to my right were two other doorways, both with metal doors. "I hope you like my humble home, it took quite a long time to finish it, and I'm still waiting on my new door. If you'll excuse me," he excused himself and walked into the kitchen, presumably to make us our tea.

I took a seat at the table, trying to figure out what was happening. I had been so angry at Odeon, yelled at him, and he was calm and polite as could be. The more I thought about how calm he was, the angrier I got.

"Are you okay?" Sylor asked me quietly.

"I don't know," I whispered. "He's supposed to be

SYLOR 183

dead, and here he is, living well and looking happy. It makes no sense."

"Perhaps he'll explain when he returns with our tea," Sylor suggested.

"Oh, I'll make him explain even if he doesn't want do." Yeah, I was angry with him. I wasn't going to let him get away with conning me, I was going to get the truth about what was happening.

"Here we are." Odeon came back into the room with a tray filled with breads, cheeses, and three mugs of steaming tea. "Hope this will be enough, I was actually in the market to go shopping when I saw you." He smiled politely at me as he handed me my mug. He handed a mug to Sylor before taking his own. "Drink up, drink up."

Odeon was in much better shape than I had remembered, and seemed to be happier.

That made me unhappy.

"What the hell is all this?" I demanded. "You..."

Odeon held up his hand to stop me. "I understand that you're confused, and that your confusion is causing you to lose your calm and to act out. Please, enjoy some bread and cheese and try to calm down."

"Calm down! What the hell are you talking about?" I yelled. "I think I've got the right to be a bit angry and to lose my calm. You were supposed to be dead, and then I find you here, alive? What the fuck, Odeon?"

He took a deep breath and set down his tea. "First," he started, his voice beginning to pick up that tone he had with me when I was younger and had made a mistake. "You will keep your voice down in my home. You are still that temperamental little woman I raised that hasn't learned how to be quiet. Secondly," he folded his hands on the table and leaned forward. "My name is no longer Odeon. I go by Viekat now. Vy-eh-kat. Understand?"

I threw my hands in the air. "Why should I give a shit about your name? Fucking tell me what is going on." My voice was shrill and was getting louder. I felt Sylor's hand on my shoulder, but I shrugged him off. "Why did you fake your death?"

Odeon, or Viekat, whatever the hell his name was, sighed and fitted me with his infamous impatient stare. "Young lady, this is my home. You will not disrespect me in my home. Do you understand me?" The calmness in his voice only infuriated me more.

I opened my mouth to yell, but Sylor spoke before me. "I believe, sir, that Nesta's confusion regarding your situation has been a bit much for her. She looked up to you, counted you as a mentor and a parental figure. You must understand the loss and now sense of betrayal that has caused her to take leave of her senses."

I stared at Sylor, my eyes hurting from how wide

they were. How in the hell could he be nice to this guy right now?

"You may very well have a valid point there. If you don't mind my asking, which one of the races are you? I haven't quite learned them all yet." Viekat...I didn't think I would ever get used to that name...put on his polite face for Sylor, one that I recognized. It was the face he usually used when he was trying to gain someone's trust right before he scammed them.

"I am a Valorni. We are a warrior race," Sylor explained. I was happy he didn't provide much more information than that.

"Ah. I understand," Viekat said with a nod. "That would make the others the Skotans and the...Kyveers?"

"K'vers. They are a very technological race. They augment themselves using technology to help gain an advantage over other species or races," Sylor said proudly. While he wasn't one of them, I knew that he had emulated them when he created the tech-sleeve he wore on his left arm, where he only had three fingers left.

I shook my head. "No."

Both of the men looked at me in confusion.

"No," I repeated. "You're not going to get away with ignoring me. I want an explanation, and I want one *now*."

"Well, at least you finally said it calmly, little mouse," Viekat said with a smile.

"Don't call me that," I growled.

He laughed. "You always did hate that nickname, didn't you?" I didn't respond. I wanted my answers and I wasn't going to let him change the subject. "Okay," he said with a clap of his hands. "I'll be straightforward with you. I needed a change."

"A change!? What the fuck do you mean, you needed a change?" I asked, surprised to hear my voice stay so calm and quiet. I decided not to be quiet anymore. "You raised me. You taught me how to steal, how to hide, and how to manipulate people. You fucking raised me, asshole!" My voice was loud, but not yet at the point of screaming. "How could you just abandon me like that? How could you abandon Sabre?"

"Don't," he said with a shake of his head. "Don't try to make this personal." He took a long drink of his tea while I fumed. How the hell was I supposed to *not* make this personal?

He continued. "Sabre was failing." His voice was stern and quiet. He was no longer interested in hearing my demands. "Sabre was falling apart, there was nothing left for me to do with it. I was close to disbanding it anyway."

"What?"

He nodded. "Yeah, it was done. The people of

Nyheim were starting to get used to our games anyway, so when the Xathi attacked, I took the opportunity to get out and start over. I knew certain people wouldn't just let me leave, so I faked my death, had a little work done, changed my name, and came here."

He raised his hands and moved them to have us take in the entire building. "I could never have had a place like this back at Nyheim. I won't apologize for making my life better and creating a better business."

"But," I said, my voice shaking, "why did you leave me?"

"That was my one regret," he said, his voice almost a whisper. His eyes dropped and he seemed to shake a little as he took in a breath. When he brought his head up, his eyes looked red. "When the Xathi attacked, you were on a run and I couldn't find you. I wanted to bring you with me, but I couldn't wait for long. I had to act. I'm sorry, my dear. I really wish I could have brought you with me."

I was struck silent. He wanted to bring me along. He hadn't forgotten me. Wait. "Wait," I said out loud. "Why haven't you come for me, then?"

"I wasn't completely sure you were still alive. I had planned on sending one of my runners to Nyheim to look for you and invite you to come here, then I heard about the dome and figured there was no way to get to you." He reached across the table and took one of my hands in his own. He had never done that, at least not like this. "Stay. Here. With me."

My heart pounded. I didn't know what to say.

"Come back into business with me and I'll make you my right hand," he said when I didn't respond. I looked over to Sylor. He didn't look happy, he actually looked a little sad. I felt sad. I didn't want to leave him, but I didn't know anything about his life. I knew this life. I was good at it.

I couldn't think about him.

I needed to think about the life I had known. The life I had lost.

I waited for Sylor to say something.

To stop me. To tell me that I couldn't leave the mission.

That I couldn't leave him.

I wanted him to stop me. To tell me to turn away from my old life. I needed something from him.

He just looked at me impassively.

"Your mission is complete with me," he said.

That was it.

I was just the means to getting the toxin.

He didn't care any more about me.

I turned to Odeon.

I nodded, slowly. "Okay." Sylor's face fell.

As did my heart.

SYLOR

I was dumbfounded. After everything, she had chosen to stay with the man that had left her, that had forsaken her to start a new life under a new identity. He was lying, I was sure of it. He had no intention of being the man that she knew.

However, it had been the only life she knew and he had offered her a chance to return to it. I could not fault her for wanting to return to what was familiar.

Which made our parting all the more painful and difficult. "Are you sure you wish to stay here, with him?" I asked as we spoke quietly in a remote corner of the warren. We had come to this corner because the closest stall was nearly fifty yards away, and the closest anyone walked was nearly ten yards away. We had our privacy, at least from prying ears.

"This is my home," she said quietly. "Sort of, anyway. This is all I've ever known."

"You've known me," I interjected.

She smiled sadly. "I know, and I've loved our time together. Well, you know."

I nodded.

"But, what good would I be to you out there? You guys are fighting some sort of war against this vine creature. What would I be able to do to help?" she asked, her hands on my chest.

I gently grabbed hold of her hands. "You were the one to help me find a way out of Nyheim. You knew where to go to find the toxin. You've been a tremendous help to me."

She shook her head, a single tear threatening to fall from her eye. "That's just it, that was all I knew. I don't have anything left to offer."

"You know that's not true," I countered. "I thought we were getting to be close."

She turned her face down, her voice slightly muffled as she spoke to the ground. "We were, and I don't want it to end, but...this is where I belong."

I could feel that I wasn't going to change her mind. I kissed the top of her head and pulled her in close to me.

"I'm going to miss you," she whispered. She turned her head up towards me. "I'll come visit you, I promise. And you need to come visit me."

I nodded. "I will," I whispered, not trusting my voice.

"And you have to tell me how the toxin works. I mean, if it's successful or not, okay?" She pulled away from me and looked up. "Come back here if it doesn't work and I'll help you find another solution, I promise."

"I will," I said, surprising myself at how strong my voice sounded. I had fully expected it to be husky, or broken, but it came out strong and certain. I did wish to return to see her. I leaned down and kissed her, one last time. When we finally parted, her eyes were filled with tears.

She pulled herself away from me and left.

Well.

I made my way back above ground. The sun was already making its way towards setting, marking the time at mid-afternoon, or later. I had a long walk ahead of me.

I started toward the forest, thinking about all that had transpired over the last few days, my thoughts circling, doing a poor job of distracting me from the ache in my gut.

I had come to trust Nesta. My feelings for her had grown into something that was important to me. I felt certain as to her capabilities. I trusted in her ability to take care of herself.

It was *him* that I did not trust.

I knew, deep down, that Odeon was a liar. He was conniving, deceitful, and about as trustworthy as a Xathi.

I had turned myself around, twice, within Duvest's city limits in confusion. Now, I turned myself around again and started heading back towards Duvest and Nesta. She needed me, and I needed her.

I no longer simply wanted her, I needed her. Her absence was a tangible thing. This wasn't logic. But it was fact.

As I got to the edge of the forest, I stopped. What had I been doing? What had I been thinking? She was a strong, stubborn, amazing woman that had survived for nineteen years in a dangerous underground environment.

She would be able to handle things...so I hoped.

I turned back around and headed back to Nyheim, determined to put my duty first. If Nesta wanted to return to the life she'd had before me, then I would return to my life before her. I had the toxin that was needed, I had to return it to Tella and Leena.

I respected Nesta, trusted her.

I needed to trust myself.

My trip back to Nyheim took several hours, it was after midnight when I returned to the hole. I lowered myself down, dropping the last couple of feet and landing heavily. The last time I was in here, Nesta had been curled into a ball, shaking uncontrollably. It had been that moment, that bit of vulnerability that had caused me to treat her differently. I started to treat her as a person, not as a common thief.

It was because of that change that I had begun to have feelings for her, that I had come to trust and believe in her. I shook my head to clear it. I couldn't think of her any longer. I had my duty to attend to. I crawled out of the tunnel and made my way quietly through the underground. I found my way back to the surface and began to make my way towards General Rouhr's office.

My only problem was that it was far too early in the morning. Everyone was asleep, and it would be inconsiderate to rouse them. They would be better suited to do their work with a full night's rest.

So I entered his building, greeted the night guard, and sat down on a bench.

"Should I notify the general that you're here?" one of the guards asked.

I shook my head 'no' and stayed sitting on the bench.

I had a long time to think about everything before the general arrived, a bit startled to find me sitting on a bench in the entrance to his office building.

"When did you get in?" he asked as he strode into the building and past me.

I rose from my seat and stepped in line, directly behind him. "A few hours ago, sir. I did not wish to wake you that early in the morning."

From the movement of his head, I could tell that he had rolled his eyes. "Punishing yourself again for something?"

"No, sir. Merely attempting to be considerate, sir," I responded. He led me to his office, motioning for me to sit. I took the chair he indicated and sat. I reached into my pack and removed the case with the toxin.

"Is that what you went looking for?" he asked as he sat at his desk.

"It is, sir," I answered as I placed the case on his desk. He stared at it for a moment, then looked back at me.

"Report."

"Nesta and I made our way to Duvest and spoke with a local herbalist. She directed us to a set of caverns where a creature called a Kouldarc lurked. Its teeth excrete the toxin, it's how they kill their prey. I managed to kill one of the beasts with a modified round of my blaster. Nesta extracted the teeth before the creature was able to disintegrate," I explained.

"Disintegrate? Really?" he asked in wonder.

"Aye, sir. It turned to dust right before our eyes," I said with a nod.

"And what happened after that?" he asked.

I hesitated as I took a deep breath. "We left the caverns and began our return."

He leaned back in his chair and folded his arms across his chest. "Did you put her back in her cell when you returned?"

I was forced to shake my head in answer. "No, sir. During our return, she managed to escape. I was unable to locate her and made the decision to return with the toxin. I felt it was the more prudent decision."

He smiled knowingly. I doubted that he believed my amended report, but it did not matter. The important matter at hand was that the toxin got to Leena and Tella, soon.

"Well, that is true. Take the toxin to the ladies, then get some rest," he ordered.

"Aye, sir." I stood, gently picked up the case, and gathered the rest of my gear.

"Actually," Rouhr said, stopping me. "Why don't you take a few days off? You've been busy and look as though you deserve it."

"I thank you, sir," I said as I lowered my head, "but I must decline. I will take this to Doctor Leena and Tella and provide them with whatever information they need from me. After a few hours of sleep, I will return to duty. Sir."

"Are you sure?" he asked. "You look exhausted."

"I understand, sir, but my duties call," I answered. "I must attend to them."

He gave a sort of half-shrug and gave a resigned sigh. "Alright. If you won't take the time off, then provide the women with the toxin and whatever information they need, then get some rest. I expect you to work on some sort of delivery device for the toxin."

"I will, sir." I left his office and took the toxin to the laboratory. Inside the lab, I presented Leena and Tella with the toxin, warning them to be careful, the teeth were still dangerous.

I answered all of their questions regarding the Kouldarc and the extraction of the teeth, including what I was able to discern of the caverns in which it lived, but ignored any questions they had about Nesta.

When they were satisfied with the information I had provided, I left them and went to my quarters. I cleaned myself off, washing away all the dirt and dust, then laid myself down in bed.

I wondered about Nesta before falling asleep.

NESTA

I had thought that things were going to go back to how they were back when Sabre was my life. I could have been more wrong, but I don't think by much.

Back when Odeon was running Sabre, we took care of the people that worked with us. Basically, we scammed the surface people that weren't poor and used the resources we got from them—sometimes legally, most times not—to take care of Sabre and everyone that worked with us. We had been, maybe not exactly family, but close to it.

We never resorted to violence unless it was in self-defense, and even then, we tried to make sure that the violence was only enough to get away, not to cause any real harm. If anyone went 'off the reservation,' as Odeon put it, and caused a lot of damage, a lot of harm, they were dealt with. They were ostracized, shunned, and—in extreme cases—turned over to the authorities on the surface.

But, no matter what, we took care of each other and only messed with the people that had the means to survive our wheeling, dealing, and scamming.

Yeah.

That wasn't the case anymore. Odeon had changed and I didn't like it. I wasn't happy with the way he was running things now. He went after everyone, even the people that trusted him. He smiled in their faces, told them all the right things, then still did what was best for him. He had me working with one of his goons, some guy so ugly, I didn't even bother remembering his name, and had sent us out into the warrens to collect.

We collected 'payment' from several people, and most of them looked as though the 'payment' was all they had left. When I brought it up with Odeon, he just shrugged at me. "Everyone needs to pay. We can no longer afford sympathy," and then he would send me on my way.

I was already struggling with the new direction he was taking things, but when he sent me after Gamma Prym, that was the last straw. Goon-boy walked with me, not telling me where we were going. He just said,

"We're getting payment," and left it at that. It drove me nuts.

When we got to Gamma Prym's door, I was on the verge of rage. "Go in, get payment, come out. Keep it simple, don't be stupid," he told me as he pushed me towards Gamma's door.

I didn't want to go in, but I did. "My darling Nesta. How are you, sweetie?" Prym said to me as I walked in, closing the door behind me. "Did you and your big green friend get what you were looking for?"

I nodded apprehensively as I made my way towards Prym's counter. "We did, Gamma. Thank you for telling us where to go." I tried to keep my voice calm and friendly.

She must have known something was up. "What is it, dear? What's the matter?"

It was better to be straightforward and not pull punches. So, I asked her outright. "What kind of business do you have with Odeon?"

"Who?"

That's right, he had changed his name here. "Sorry," I said. "I meant Viekat."

Her expression hardened. "Don't tell me you work for him."

"I do, maybe. I'm not completely sure anymore," I admitted.

She was angry, and I couldn't blame her. "How

could you work for such a man? I thought you were better than that." She was disappointed in me, and that hurt. It hurt almost as much as letting Sylor go.

"He…" I started, then stopped. I looked back at the door, then got closer to Prym, my voice lowered so only she could hear me. "He didn't used to be this way. I didn't know he worked this way now."

"You mean he's conned and bullied people before?" she asked.

"Not exactly," I shrugged. "Sort of, actually." I gave her the abridged version of how he raised me and how we ran Sabre before the Xathi attack, including what he told me when I found him here.

"So, are you going to keep working for him then?" she asked, a hopeful look in her eyes. She stared me down as I hesitated. I blushed a bit, causing her to smile.

"No. I think I'm done with him," I smiled. Then my smile faded. "But, one of his goons is right outside."

"The ugly one or the tall one?"

"Ugly one," I answered, trying not to laugh.

She grimaced. "He's a mean one." She let out a heavy sigh and reached under her counter, pulling out a small bundle of money. "Here's this month's payment."

"No," I said desperately. "I'll figure something out."

She shook her head. "No, you won't, not with how

he is now. If what you told me is true, your mentor has changed. He's more dangerous now. He won't hesitate to hurt people, he's done it before." She shoved the money into my hands. "Take it, give it to him. Then get out. Make sure you get out, and if you come back here…and I hope you do, I miss you…stay away from him."

I nodded and hugged her. I was breaking away when Ugly slammed open the door. "What's taking so long?"

"Nothing," I lied. "We were talking. What, you got a date or something?"

"Shut up," he snarled. "Did the old bat pay you?"

I never thought I could desire to beat someone so badly, but when he said that, I had a quick fantasy of beating on his face until he was pretty.

"I paid her," Prym shot back loudly. "Now, get out of my shop."

I shrugged and walked towards Ugly as he tried to stare Prym down. If he only knew about the blaster she had under her counter, he might act differently. He growled at me as he snatched the money from my hands and walked out. I shot a quick look back at Gamma Prym, winked at her, and left.

That night, I packed my stuff.

I couldn't do this anymore.

This wasn't what I had signed up for.

Odeon always went to sleep early and he posted a guard outside his door. I waited till I could hear him snoring and then I peeked outside.

The guard, after a bit, went to go fetch some food. There wasn't much to really guard against. And he wasn't expecting that I would be trying to escape.

But still, I knew I had only a small amount of time.

As soon as the guard left, I tiptoed to the door. I looked back one last time.

It held nothing more me. I had made such a mistake in staying behind.

Without looking back, I left. Well, I did something first. I stole back Gamma's money, and made sure that I put a little bit of fish oil in Odeon's booze. I knew he was allergic to fish, so this would at least make him sick as hell. Bastard deserved worse, but I wasn't a cold-blooded killer.

Now, if he happened to 'accidentally' drink too much and die of an allergic reaction, that wouldn't be my fault.

I made my way back to Nyheim. Traveling the pathways at night wasn't the smartest thing in the world for me to do, but I had done it before, so I knew what to look and listen for. I didn't have any problems making it back, just worn out legs and a tired mind was all.

The sun was barely peeking above the horizon when

I got back to the dome. I walked around it until I found the hole Sylor had dug, still in the dark due to the dome. That tiny, small, miniscule, enclosed hole that was too tight and would cave in on top of me, burying me forever.

There wasn't enough air.

There wasn't enough room.

There wasn't enough...

I had started hyperventilating. I couldn't just sit here, and there was no other way to get in. I forced my breathing to calm down and knelt down by the hole. I slowly, carefully, stupidly put my foot down into the hole and found a foothold. I lowered myself, like an idiot, into the hole, fighting the completely rational panic that was taking over.

I took a deep breath, then took four more, took an even deeper breath, and held it as I scrambled down. The instant my feet touched bottom, I dropped down to my hands and knees and crawled as fast as I could until I was out. I finally started breathing again as I hunched over in one of those awkward yoga poses some of the women did.

I wasn't sure how long I stayed there cursing myself for being stupid enough to go alone through the tunnel, praising myself for managing a way through, and swearing that I would *never*, ever, ever, ever do that again.

I made my way into the small warrens. I made sure to pass along the news that Odeon was alive and well, sort of, in the Duvest underground, making a living while we starved and suffered.

Many of them were angry and wanted revenge. I told them it wasn't worth it, we needed to take care of ourselves. A few suggested rebuilding Sabre, and one of them recommended me. When I asked why, they said it was because I had come to know the aliens and made friends with one.

"If we rebuild, maybe we can do something about that traitorous bastard that left us," one of the older ones said.

"Yeah, we can take over his operation there," another said. That started a small flood of people and members wanting to rebuild and conquer. I shot them all down, told them that we had to be better.

"Then stay, work with us, help us rebuild," one more said, her voice scratchy.

"I will," I said. "But I have something to do first."

I headed above ground. I had to see Sylor. I wasn't sure where he would be, so when I saw one of the guards that I had recognized, I asked.

He looked like he didn't want to answer me, but I was resolute in my demands. Basically, I didn't let him go and annoyed the hell out of him until he finally told me, most likely to shut me up and to get away from me.

"He's in the armory. Has been for maybe two days. Can I go now?" He wasn't happy with me. He gave me directions and stomped away, obviously annoyed.

I didn't bother hiding my smile.

But there was something I needed to do.

Sylor

"Skrell," I grumbled, looking down at the broken circuit board on the table. I had been trying to figure out the best way to build a delivery device for the toxin, but it was getting harder and harder to focus. I had been at it since the crack of dawn, and still no progress.

Stretching my back, I paced the entirety of the workshop as I tried to think of something that could help. The harder I thought, though, the more my mind insisted on circling back to Nesta. I worried about her safety, especially since I knew she had stayed with that arrogant little man.

I found it harder to believe Nesta was loyal to such a

man, but I had little understanding of the way human families behaved. It didn't make it easier that Odeon wasn't biologically related to Nesta, of course. But he had raised her, and so that had to count for something.

Returning to the table, I exhaled sharply and pushed the broken pieces of the board onto the trash. Then, grabbing some new circuitry, I held the soldering gun and got to work. It was a delicate procedure, but most days I wouldn't have had any trouble doing something like this. But, after finding and losing Nesta, it felt as if my skills had abandoned me.

"Skrell," I hissed through gritted teeth, frustration getting the best of me. Somehow, I had connected the wrong circuits and, in the process, rendered another circuit board useless. I threw it in the trash harshly, and was about to pick up a new board when I heard something that made me pause.

"Man, you suck at your job," I heard someone laugh right behind me, the softness of that voice making my heart stop beating for a second. Barely believing my ears, I turned around and... there she was.

Nesta stood at the other end of the workshop, casually leaning against the doorway. She had her arms folded over her chest, and there was a bright smile on her crimson lips. I blinked, unsure if what I was seeing was real.

"Is that really you?" I asked her, slowly lowering the soldering gun.

"No," she laughed once more. "I'm the general." With that, she pushed herself off the doorway and rushed toward me. I opened my arms by instinct and she fell into them as if she had never left in the first place. "God, I missed you," she whispered, her head against my chest.

"Nesta...what are you doing here?" I asked. "I thought you had decided to stay."

"And I did," she nodded, looking up into my eyes. "But I was wrong about Odeon. He isn't the person I thought he was. I just couldn't stay there. Besides, I knew you'd be useless without me."

"That is true," I said, now it being my turn to laugh. I knew she was just joking, but she was right. Without her by my side I was completely useless. I couldn't concentrate, I couldn't sleep...I couldn't *live*. Somehow, this tiny human had asserted herself as the axis around which my life spun.

"I'm sorry I didn't come back with you, Sylor."

"You don't have to apologize, little one," I found myself saying, holding her close. After being without her, I was almost afraid of letting go. "You're here now."

"Yes, I am," she whispered, going on her tiptoes to brush her lips against mine. I closed my eyes as we kissed, one hand on the nape of her neck as I held her.

She felt so tiny against my body, so delicate, and that was enough to awaken my innermost protective instincts. But more than just feeling protective toward Nesta, I also felt a certain...possessiveness.

I wanted her to be *mine*.

"I missed this," I said, both hands now on her hips. Moving fast, I pushed her back and pinned her against the wall. I leaned in, bringing my mouth down onto her neck, and I kissed her smooth skin as she moaned weakly into my ear.

"Not as much as I've missed this," she purred, flattening her hand between my legs. The pressure of her hand was enough to make me become even harder than I already was, boiling blood rushing through my veins at breakneck speed.

"Then we have to do something about it, don't we?" I asked, taking a step back. Without taking my eyes off her, I reached for my datapad on the table and tapped the screen a few times. The door to the room slammed shut almost immediately, and a red light over the doorway indicated it had been locked.

"Good thinking," she chuckled, swaying her hips as she moved toward me. Laying both hands on my chest, she then lowered herself until her knees touched the floor. She kept looking into my eyes as she unbuttoned my pants and pushed them down, freeing my erection.

I gritted my teeth as she grabbed my hard cock, and

I couldn't stop myself from exhaling sharply as she ran the tip of her tongue down my whole length. When she finally parted her lips and took me inside her mouth, I was so out of it I wasn't sure I could remember my own name.

I had never experienced intercourse with a human before Nesta, but now...Nesta had become an addiction. Nothing I had ever experienced compared to the way her body made me feel.

"So good," I let out as she bobbed her head, her lips running up and down the length of my hardness. I laid both hands on her head and, allowing instinct to kick in, I started directing her movements while I thrusted. I would've gone all the way, but I needed more than just her mouth. Taking a deep breath, I beat my own body into submission and slid out from her mouth.

"More," I growled as I pulled her up to her feet. Grabbing her by the hips, I picked her up effortlessly and sat her down on the edge of my workstation. I swept whatever was on top of it to the floor and hurriedly kicked off my boots, eager to have her naked body against mine. I was about to reach for her clothes when she stopped me, one hand on my chest.

"Easy," she chuckled teasingly. "Don't rip those. You don't want me walking out of here naked, do you?" Taking her shirt off as I busied myself with pushing her pants down her legs, I somehow kept my urges at bay...at least until she was in her underwear.

"You can walk out of here without *this*," I said, hooking my fingers on her scrap of cloth that covered her loins and ripping it off her body. She squealed and said something then, but my heart was beating so loudly inside my chest that I didn't even hear what it was. I just pushed her knees apart and closed the space between us, my mouth crashing against hers urgently.

She reached down for me as we kissed and, angling my cock down, she pressed its tip right against her entrance. "Easy now," she whispered against my lips, and I used all of my willpower not to thrust savagely. I slid inside of her carefully, enjoying the way her inner walls tightly hugged my length, and I only stopped when she dug her fingernails into my chest. "Good," she said, "you can do easy. Now I want *hard*."

I said nothing.

I merely grinned and got to work.

Holding her tightly, I started thrusting as hard as I could. I cupped one of her breasts as I did it, and leaned in to suck her perky nipple into my mouth. The taste of her body was maddening, and it just made me want to ravage her even harder. And that's exactly what I did.

"Fuck me, Sylor," she moaned, her fingernails digging into my chest like daggers. I didn't even feel the pain. I just concentrated on her expression of pure ecstasy and on the way her inner walls became tighter and tighter, squeezing my thickness like a vise.

"There's nothing I want more than that," I told her, weaving my fingers into her hair. I held her gaze as I thrusted, the sound of flesh on flesh echoing throughout the room, and I only changed gears when Nesta closed her eyes. Her eyelids fluttered quickly, and her body became so tense that I became worried for a fraction of a second.

And then she screamed.

Her high-pitched voice hung in the room from one second to the next, the sound of it brimming with pleasure. I just took in the expression on her face, one of pure ecstasy, and surrendered to the sweet release my body craved.

Gritting my teeth, I thrust one final time.

And, just like that, I exploded.

Fire climbed up my spine in an inferno, and whatever rationality still existing in my mind was burned to a crisp as I came. Breathing hard, my body still reeling from the experience, I just wrapped my arms around Nesta and pulled her against me.

"I can't believe you're back," I whispered into her ear, still not believing her naked skin was against mine.

"I had to," she replied softly. Resting her forehead against mine, she offered me a little smile. "Life without you...it's just not any fun."

NESTA

"You are an interesting little one, aren't you?" the alien named Rouhr said as I sat in his office. His red eyes were disconcerting. They seemed to stare right through me all the way down to the beginnings of my bloodlines, wherever—and whenever—the hell that was.

He was a big man, but only slightly bigger than Sylor, which meant that they both towered over me and made me seem like a tiny little teenager. Then again, I had just stopped being in my teens, if you believed the birthdate Odeon had told me, and was still pretty tiny.

Rouhr's red skin was so much different than Sylor's. Sylor's skin was a deep, rich, vibrant green that was full of youth. Rouhr's was a faded red that spoke to his age, and, I was going to guess, his experiences. His scarred arms told so many stories that I wanted to know, but didn't think it was my place to ask, at least not now.

"Thank you? Sir?" I responded. I wasn't sure if he had complimented me or not.

He chuckled a bit. "Relax. Everything is cleared up. You've been pardoned, no record of your transgression. The old lady isn't even angry at you, she said that she knows what it's like to survive on next to nothing."

That made me feel better.

"Combined with what you and Sylor have told me about your excursion, as well as your connection to the people underground, I have a proposal for you," he said.

"What did you have in mind, sir?"

"I want you to be a liaison between those of us on the surface and those below." He took a drink from his water glass before continuing. "I'd rather have them all back above ground, but I can understand if they wish to stay below. It's hard to change what you're used to." His tone led me to believe that he wasn't just talking about the people below. I knew that Rouhr and the others landed here in a ship, found another one, and were now living here. I was pretty damn sure he was talking about himself and his people as well as mine.

"You want me to be, what, a go-between for you and the underground?"

"In a sense," he answered, his head bobbing up and down a bit as he did so. "You have shown that there are some serious skills owned by your people, and if we work together, we can all help one another. If the toxin...we really need to name that stuff...if it works, then we might be able to bring the dome down. If it comes down, we can return to rebuilding Nyheim.

"Along with the rebuild, we can start growing and farming again. We'll help your people eat, as well as with whatever can only be found up top, you help us with whatever we need that can only be found below ground," he finished.

I was pretty confident we could make it happen. "Okay," I said. "I think we can work with that."

"Good. One caveat, however," he said.

"What's that?"

He looked me square in the eyes, his look stern to show me he meant business. "There will be no illegal activities by your people. I will not hesitate to have them arrested and charged."

I shook my head and held up my hands. "No worries there, General. If I'm in charge of Sabre, I won't run it anything like Odeon did. I want to make sure our people are cared for, not hustled."

"Good," he said with a nod. "Once you've run this by your people, and you've figured out your command structure, we'll negotiate trade and everything else we need to make this a success."

"Works for me," I said. I reached over to his desk and grabbed the glass of water he had poured for me when I first came in. I took a drink, relishing how cold the water still was.

"Very well," he stood up, an indication the meeting was over. I stood up as well. "Thank you for your help, Nesta. We would not have been able to get through this without you." He held out his hand.

I took it and shook it, probably trying a little too hard to be firm with it. "Glad I could help. I'll go talk to the underground and present your idea. I don't think it'll be much of a problem, though."

"I hope not. Thank you, again," he said as he led me to his office door and walked me out. I left his office, walked down the hall, waved at Tobias, and left.

About twenty minutes later, I was back underground with word going out that I was calling for a general meeting. A general meeting was basically a get-together where things were announced, sometimes voted on, and mostly a reason for everyone to be in one place to get drunk.

Within an hour, the people I needed there were there, as were so many more. Of the nearly three hundred of us that lived underground, I counted only a few dozen that weren't there.

"What do you have to tell us?" a voice called out. I looked towards its source to see Topan standing with Stupid Joe. Joe still glared at me, even though I doubted he knew why he was angry with me. Topan actually smiled and nodded towards me.

"Well," I started. "General Rouhr, the alien boss guy in charge up there, has offered us a deal. Since we have access to weird, crazy, and rare things that they don't up there, he wants to form a partnership with us."

"Why should we do that?" a voice from the back yelled out.

I raised my voice a little louder so they could hear me everywhere. "Well, as soon as the vines are down, they can go back to growing their crops and raising their livestock. They'll trade with us, which means food."

"Ah, he's probably lying to you," another voice yelled out. I looked over at the owner of said voice and wasn't really that surprised to see that old man Samuel had said it.

"Really, Samuel? And what do you know about truth?" I fired back. That brought a lot of laughs from the crowd and made Samuel get red-faced. But, he shut up and that was what I wanted. I turned back to the crowd. "Look, I don't want to run things the way Odeon did. I want all of us to work together to help each other. If you have a skill, or know something, or know where to find something, we need to know. It might help us when we deal with above ground."

"What about the vines?" a female voice asked.

"They're working on that. We got some Kouldarc venom. They're studying it right now and trying to find a way to get it into the vine," I answered. When I had mentioned the Kouldarc, there were a lot of sudden nods of admiration and a few 'oohs' and 'aahs'. "Look, I want to make sure we all take care of one another and do better, and this is a way to do it. We need them, we really do." It was true, the above-grounders had the food. "And, depending on what it is, they need us."

"What if we don't have anything?" Stupid...no, shouldn't call him that anymore, I need to be better. Ahem, Joe asked.

"That's just it, we do. How many herbs have we discovered down here that aren't available up top?" I asked the crowd. I went on, not waiting for their answer. "We also got some of the prisms a few of you use, and, most importantly, we have a way out in case the venom doesn't work. If the venom doesn't work, the people up top are probably going to start wanting to leave, and right now, we have the exit."

"Why are we even talking about this?" Topan yelled out above the crowd. He picked his way through the crowd and jumped up on the small dais I was standing on. He winked at me. "Look, Nesta has brought us a proposition, and I think most of us agree that it's a good one. Should we vote to approve it?"

Without even calling for a vote, most of the crowd raised their left hand high in the air, a vote for 'yes.' Topan nodded knowingly. "Well, then the only thing left is to pick someone to lead us and make sure that everything that deals with up above is done right."

"Who, you?" Samuel called out derisively.

"Nope. Nesta."

I knew that's what General Rouhr wanted, but it still felt good to hear my name. The crowd started clapping and whistling, even Joe and Samuel joined in. They wanted me to be in charge.

"Well, kiddo," Topan said in my ear so I could hear him over the cheering. "Looks like you get to show us the right way to do things." He took a step back, gave me a short bow, and came up smiling and clapping.

I was overwhelmed. I had dreamt of this, but never like this. I always figured that if I took over Sabre, it would be after Odeon's retirement and when I was a *lot* older. I was nervous, to be honest. What the hell did I know about being a boss and running things? What the hell did I know about being a liaison and negotiating between two groups of people?

Oh well, guess I didn't have much of a choice.

Whatever I needed to learn, I'd learn on the job. It felt good to have everyone liking and respecting me. It was almost like I finally had my family back, minus the overbearing asshole that Odeon was.

Everything was perfect.

Almost.

SYLOR

A week had passed since my return to Nyheim and the beginnings of Leena's study of the toxin, which they had come to name Phokite. As they were studying it, and making a synthetic version of it, I had been busy, as well.

During my time in the armory, I had taken apart four different rifles and used the various parts to build a new dart gun. During testing, the gun was able to put a dart nearly six inches into a rubber composite that Takar had made of the vine. While it wasn't, in my opinion, a viable replacement for the vine, it did give me an idea about the capabilities of the gun and the darts that I had made.

I spent a few days attempting to increase the power

output, and the next set of tests put the dart nearly an entire foot into the composite.

When I wasn't working on the gun or the darts, I was with Nesta, helping her with the recreation of Sabre and the trade negotiations between the underground and the upper levels of Nyheim.

Nesta's return had been a moment of jubilation and enjoyment. I don't believe I had ever felt as happy as I was when she had come back. She had spent a lot of time working with the general, learning how to lead and how to deal with politics. I was unsure of how much she could learn in only a week, but her venture with me and her discovery of Odeon's lies had endeared her to her people.

Besides, she was a natural, so I was assuming that she was merely learning nuances of the leadership game.

"Hey!"

I snapped my head up and looked away from my workbench to where the sound had come from. Tella was standing in the armory doorway, arms crossed and looking cross.

"Seriously, are you deaf?" she asked me.

"No, no I am not. My apologies," I returned. "I was preoccupied with the modifications to the gun."

"No shit," she snapped as she came into the armory, my small case in her hands. "Here," she said as she placed the case gently on my workbench. "Here's the Phokite you brought back from Duvest. We've finished analyzing and synthesizing it."

"I thank you," I said with a grateful nod.

"Yeah, yeah. Listen and watch, okay," she said. Despite her relationship with Rokul, she still seemed to be short with the rest of us, or at least with me. "To put the Phokite into your darts, you want to do this." She opened the case and took out one of the vials of the original toxin. She took a small needle tip from the case and attached it to the vial. She then took the vial, grabbed one of my darts, and inserted the vial, making sure to put the small needle tip into the dart tip. "Now, when you fire it, it'll compress and release the toxin."

"Thank you again," I said. I proceeded to take the last three vials and repeated her technique.

"Good work," she commented nicely. I flashed her a quick look. "Okay, okay, I'm not always a bitch, you know."

"Oh, yes, yes, I am well aware of that," I said, smiling. "Rokul has commented numerous times on how nice you are."

She looked at me in wide-eyed horror. She was truly speechless for the first time since I had made her acquaintance, and I savored the moment.

It did not last long however, as I was unable to

maintain my composure and started to convulse with barely repressed laughter.

She caught on quickly and punched me in the shoulder. "You asshat," she said without any of her normal malice towards me. "I can't believe you just did that to me."

I shrugged. "I did tell you that I was not always so… how did you put it…prim and proper?"

"Okay, okay. You got me," she smiled. She quickly sobered and looked me in the eyes. "Good luck. I hope it works this time."

"As do I," I agreed.

"Oh, you do know that this wasn't the toxin we originally sent you for, don't you?" she asked.

I was taken aback. "I'm sorry, what did you say?"

She nodded and smiled. "Yeah, we were hoping for the Narrissi extract. It's from a plant. You brought us something different."

"Then, how do we know this will work?" I asked. How could we have retrieved the wrong thing?

"Whoa there, prim-n-proper. Hold your horses," she said. What were horses? "This stuff is twice as potent as the Narrissi extract, so if this doesn't work, the Narrissi extract wouldn't have done anything."

The wave of relief that came over me was like a cold shower on a hot day. "Please do not cause me such anxiety like that again," I said politely.

"Really?"

"What?" I asked.

"You just bullshitted me as a joke, and now you're all proper and eloquent again," she started. "Why can't you just talk normally with me?"

I nodded in understanding. "In that case, I offer you my apologies. I have been speaking like this for so long, that it is difficult for me to speak any other way." I leaned back on my stool. "But, if you want me to speak plain, then I will."

"Oh?" she asked, crossing her arms and smirking.

"Well," I started with a half-shrug, "you have been a very difficult human to work with, and I don't really understand what I've done to deserve it. But," I put up a hand to stop her from commenting, "I like you. You're good for Rokul, and you've gotten his pain-in-the-ass... I said that right, yes?"

She nodded.

"You got his pain-in-the-ass brother to stop being such an ass. Takar is finally interesting and fun to be around," I finished.

"Thanks." She smiled at me as she playfully punched me in the shoulder before she left. I, in turn, loaded the darts into the clip, snapped the clip into the dart gun, and after making sure the safety was still on, left the armory and made my way towards where we had conducted all of our other tests.

Along the way, General Rouhr, Strike Team One, and my team joined me.

"You gonna flame out horribly?" Sakev smirked. I flashed him a death look, then winked. The shock and confusion on his face was enough for me. Let him figure out what I meant.

"Sakev has a semi-valid question," Vrehx commented. "What are your thoughts on this one?"

I shrugged. "I'm not entirely sure, but this is the best bet we have. If this fails, we're going to have to start taking people out through the tunnels below."

"Well," Axtin cut in, "at least we have a back-up plan."

"That we do," Rouhr said. "Your friend has been a remarkable leader and liaison already. We've already gotten permission to use the tunnels if necessary, as well as a plan to get to Duvest. Since communications are back, we can talk to the people of Duvest. Apparently, someone named Viekat has been imprisoned and a Gamma Prym now runs the Duvest underground."

"Really?" I remarked. "That is fantastic."

"That it is," came a voice from behind Rokul. Nesta peeked her head out from behind him and smiled at me. She made her way through to me and immediately snaked her arm around mine. "With Gamma and me coordinating things with Rouhr and Duvest's bosses, we have a place to go."

I looked down at her and smiled. "I'm glad."

We arrived at the testing site, the home to eighteen-plus colossal failures to find a way out. This would be attempt number nineteen on my part, twenty-one in total counting Rokul and Takar's two attempts. I took a deep breath as everyone held back. I stopped within two yards of the vine, clicked off the safety, and brought the rifle up to my shoulder.

There was no way for me to miss, but I didn't risk it. I took aim, lining up my sights and controlled my breathing. I took a deep breath, held it, and let it out slowly as I gently squeezed the trigger.

Time seemed to slow. It's an interesting sensation what you notice when time stops. The tiny, almost imperceptible breeze moving a leaf on the vine just slightly. The wrinkles and slight discolorations of the vine that made it different from the other vines around it, even how much effort I subconsciously used to blink and how dark my life became for the briefest of moments as my eyelids shut.

The dart flew towards the vine, piercing the air with simplicity as it headed towards its target. The dart hit and embedded itself deep within the vine, the puncture mark almost closing in on itself with the power of the dart.

Nothing happened. I counted three hundred heartbeats and nothing happened.

"Welp," I heard Sakev's voice fill the air. "That sucked. Who's hungry? I wanna eat something *big* before I go crawling through tunnels and stuff."

"Shut up, Sakev," Axtin said.

"What? Really? We have to be quiet right now?" Sakev fought back.

"SHUT UP!" the two teams said collectively. I felt Nesta's hands on my arm and heard her taking a breath in. Before she could speak, I stepped forward and looked intently at the puncture mark. It was turning gray.

After another one hundred heartbeats, the gray began to spread and the vine started to shrivel. "MOVE!" I yelled as the vine shriveled faster and began to fall. There was a thunderous 'thwump' behind me as Nesta and I ran. I looked back to see maybe twenty feet of green vine had fallen off and crashed to the ground while the rest turned to a gray, shriveled husk.

"Ah, hahaha," I cried out in joy. I grabbed Nesta, picked her up, and kissed her passionately. I couldn't care less if the others saw us. I heard the teams cheering. Whether they were cheering my kiss or the death of the vine, I wasn't sure and I didn't care.

"We have an answer," I said breathlessly as Nesta and I separated.

"We need to start calculating trajectories to shoot so that the vines fall outward, so we don't have collateral damage," Sakev said.

We all looked at him.

"That is very true," I replied. "I'm impressed."

He shrugged. "I can think seriously from time to time."

People went back to cheering and making plans. We slapped each other's backs and gave shouts of victory.

I turned back to Nesta.

She had a smile on her face as she came back to me.

"I'm so proud of you," she said. "So proud." She brought her lips to mine once again and I kissed her until our lips were raw.

And still, I wanted more.

NESTA

So much had happened during the last week, I never got around to really figuring out where I was going to live. During the last week, I basically slept wherever I could find a bed because I had been so busy trying to restart Sabre with a proper management structure and real leadership.

I had spent the last three days negotiating with Rouhr about trade and services that both sides would provide for one another if we managed to get the dome down.

Then, yesterday, Sylor tried the toxin. I found the name that the girls had given it to be hilarious. It was called Phokite, but if you weren't paying attention or it was said too fast, it sounded a bit like 'fuck-it,' and that was funny. Anyway, he tried the toxin and it had worked. The first vine he had shot withered and fell.

We didn't have a way out, not yet, since it was an interior vine, but he fired off the last three vials he had and we watched as the vines died. There was real sunlight streaming into the city now, and the ladies— what were their names? Leena and Tella, I think—were getting him some synthetic copies of the venom. He had been really confident that we would be able to have the vines down soon.

"Give me a week, maybe two, and we'll have the vines down and the city will be free once more," he had said while we ate dinner last night. He had looked across the table at me and smiled. He looked so happy and proud. To see him happy made me feel happy inside.

"That's good," I said. "It'll be nice to be able to walk around wherever we want to, and to get food again."

He chuckled as he took a bite of his ramen. He had taken me to a little place close to where I had shown him the way underground. With the tunnels open now and food getting through, this ramen place had begun importing food and had quickly become a local favorite.

"How are things going with Sabre?" he asked as he bit into a dumpling, immediately hissing and sucking air in. I could see the steam rising. I hid my smile behind my hand as he suffered through the bite. "I should have waited another minute before trying that."

I nodded and quickly put another bite of ramen in my mouth to hide my humor. However, I was not to be left out of the insanity. I bit down and must have bitten down into a bit of pepper, a bit of ridiculously hot pepper. I started breathing heavily and coughing. I reached for my drink and gulped it down, barely quenching the lava that was destroying the inside of my mouth.

When I was able to breathe and talk again, Sylor was laughing so hard that he had started hiccupping. That made me laugh.

Things had gone so well last night that I asked him if I could spend the night. He not only agreed, but he said that I could move in, have a permanent –sort of— home. I say 'sort of' because if the vines came back, or something else attacked, we would most likely move. But that was beside the point.

Sylor had asked me to move in with him. I was elated. I had never had a real home before. Yes, I lived in the underground and usually slept in one place, but it was never a place that I really wanted to go. Sylor's home, no matter what it looked like, I wanted to be there simply because he was there.

He had brought me to his home, a small place that was a twenty-minute walk from Rouhr's offices. It was the first house you came across when you came to the housing area, a little green place with a fence around the front yard.

It was a bit empty inside. There was furniture, but nothing personal. It was very...boring. We made love last night, and after he left for work this morning, I went to the underground to find some things for Sylor's home.

The one thing that we were good at under the surface was adaptation. We could adapt and change anything to fit what we needed it to fit. Sylor was sort of the same way. He took apart four rifles to create his new dart gun, then took the remnants of the four rifles and created a new sniper rifle for his friend Tu'ver that shot farther. The guy was simply an engineering freak.

So, I scoured the market and people's 'collections' for things that I thought Sylor would like. Weapons, parts, remade tools, anything that looked like it had been modified and changed, even if it didn't work anymore. I called in favors, opened up credit, and bought whatever I could and had some of the guys help me deliver it all to Sylor's house.

I spent the next several hours putting everything around the house, using them as decoration, trying to create a bit of a flow from room to room.

When I was done, I went to my meeting with Topan to discuss the harvesting and growing Maymoss. It grew in one of the caverns we were connected to. The cavern was lit by some sort of glow-in-the-dark stalactite that produced a semi-pleasant blue light. The blue light helped the Maymoss grow nice and thick. We used Maymoss for just about everything. It was used to make blankets, it tasted good so it was used as a vegetable in our stews, and carpeting since it seemed to grow everywhere. Some people had even started to cut some from the cavern and sort of plant it around their booths or on the streets.

That evening, I returned home—god it felt good to say that—and realized that I had beaten Sylor there. I decided to raid his kitchen and make him a dinner to go with his new toys. I was in the middle of making dinner when the door opened. I rushed out of the kitchen to see Sylor's face.

I don't think I had ever seen anyone look so happy, or surprised, all at the same time. My own cheeks began to hurt as I smiled at his joy.

"What is all this?" Sylor breathed. I could barely hear his words, but I could sense what he was asking.

"I wanted to make you feel more at home," I said as I came over and kissed his cheek. "I wanted to thank you for everything."

"What did I do?" he asked, not looking at me at all. He was still smiling and staring.

I put my arm around his lower back, it was all I could reach, and held him close. "You helped me get out of my own little hell and find my way. I have a home now, and I have a family. It's all because of you."

He looked down at me then. "Am I part of that family?"

"I would like you to be," I said quietly.

He smiled. "I would like to be, as well." He bent down and kissed me as I craned my neck. While it hurt my neck to stretch for that long, the sensation of his powerful arms wrapped around me while his lips engulfed mine made the pain worth it.

"You have always been strong, Nesta. You just needed to get away from Odeon and discover your own abilities," he said as we broke apart.

"Thank you," I said as I hugged him. "But I don't think I've ever known what it means to really feel safe until now. You make me feel safe."

"And you make me feel as though I belong," he responded. I shot a look of confusion at him. He chuckled. "I've always been the odd one in my family. I'm actually the smallest male, and the weakest. That's why I turned to technology, it kept me away from my family and their incessant need to prove everything through strength. It's why I speak the way I do."

"I love how you talk," I said. "I'm sorry about your family."

"I'm not. They made me strong, and I'm honored to be able to use that strength to make you feel safe," he said. "What is that smell?"

"Ah!" I shouted and rushed to the kitchen. I hadn't burned anything, but my sauce had boiled over. Sylor helped me finish making dinner and we had a pleasant evening. After dinner, he walked all over the house, inspecting everything. I'd noticed something about him. When he was really excited about something, his left hand twitched. I was happy to see his hand twitch a lot.

The one thing that he spent the most time with was a piece of prosthetic. It was something that one of the men down below had made to use as both protection and as extra power when he was digging. It fit over his arm, and he had modified it with several weapons and a small energy shield. The shield only lasted two seconds, but it was still there.

I could see his eyes twitching back and forth as he studied it. "This is incredible," he finally said with a breath of awe.

"I'm glad you like it," I said, proud of what I had done.

"I love it. It's beautiful."

It took me a moment to realize that he'd said it's.

Then, without realizing what was going to come out of my mouth, I said, "I love you."

He grabbed me and my feet left the ground.

"I love you, too," Sylor said.

I couldn't reply. His mouth was covering mine and his tongue danced circles with mine.

I could feel his hands unbuttoning my pants. I straightened my legs as he pulled them off. His huge hands began to caress my ass before slapping it.

I yelped in pleasure and pain.

It took two seconds for Sylor to rip my panties off. Then he lifted me up.

My pussy hovered above his face.

He brought me closer to his mouth like a toy, and stuck out his tongue.

That strong tongue, with its deft muscles, began to lap at me.

"Oh fuck," I moaned, as my eyes rolled back in their sockets.

"Let me show you how much I love you," Sylor chuckled and forcefully pushed his tongue against my clit. He rubbed it back and forth over and over until I couldn't feel my legs.

Still, I managed to wrap them around his torso.

Sylor began eating me with gusto.

As waves of pleasure began to cascade through my

body, I lost all control of my limbs. Sylor held me up and continued to flick his tongue.

I came.

Over and over.

Before I blacked out from the intense waves of pleasure.

That was a marvelous way to be told someone loved you.

SYLOR

Leena and Tella were working as fast as they could to produce the synthetic Phokite, and I made sure that their efforts were used quickly and effectively.

Every case they brought me or sent to me, I used within only fifteen minutes.

And within seven to ten minutes of every shot taken, the vines started withering, dying, and coming down. Now I wasn't killing vines in only one place, either. I was attempting to be strategic, so I was shooting vines in various places around the city.

It made sense to have multiple openings in case the Puppet Master started doing something more dangerous than sending down its tendrils. With multiple openings, people would be able to escape no matter where they were within the city.

It was a smart decision. The pieces of vines that fell, depending on condition, were then taken to the labs to be studied.

The other thing that had been sensational during the past three days was that none of the vines had grown back. The tendrils were still acting as they had been for the past several weeks, simply invading buildings and feeling around.

No one had a notion as to what the tendrils were looking for, but we were starting to not care anymore. We had a way out.

Of course, the non-optimistic members of our force had brought up something that was extremely important. The Puppet Master was still alive and we still didn't know what it wanted with us, or what the Puppet Master itself was.

Tella still had some ideas that it was an ancient creature, but we were unable to figure out how ancient.

As I fired off my last round into a vine on the north side of the city, Karzin approached me. "Afternoon."

"Sir. How are things?"

He went "Eh," and gave me a slight grin, something I had forgotten he knew how to do before Annie came into his life. "A lot of people are very happy that we've finally found a way out of the dome. Even more are happy that we're getting rid of the vines."

"But?" I asked, sensing that he was going to tell me

something leaning towards the negative.

"There are a lot of citizens, a few guards, and one of the members of Team Three that are terrified with what the creature has in store for us next. They're scared that this is just the lull before the storm, so to speak," he explained to me.

I nodded in understanding. I partially agreed. The fact that the tendrils had not resorted to attacking or defending, that the vines had not attempted to regrow, and that nothing else had happened since the first vine had been killed…it was a perplexing and frightening thought.

"They might not be wrong," Karzin said, echoing my thoughts. "There might just be something to what they're saying. Whatever this creature is, it could just be biding its time, getting us into a false sense of safety before it obliterates us all."

"Well," I said, "there is something to that. Whenever we attacked this thing before, it always seemed to either heal itself or block our attempts. Nothing worked against it. Suddenly, this has worked."

"Good point," Karzin said as we started walking back towards the offices. "What are you thinking?"

"What if Tella is correct?" I asked. "What if this is an intelligent creature and it truly is playing a game that we're woefully unprepared for?"

He snorted. "You really think this plant is that

smart?"

"What if it's not a plant?" I countered. "What if it's some sort of beast that can control vegetation?"

He looked at me as we walked. "You really believe that?"

I shrugged. "I'm not completely sure as to what I should believe, to be honest." We rounded a corner and passed by the local ramen shop. I had come to really like ramen. It was a simple meal, and with my metabolism, it was more of a snack than a meal most of the time. "Let's stop in here," I suggested, turning into the shop.

"Really? You're hungry?" he joked as he followed me in.

"I find it comforting. Helps me think," I answered. "Good afternoon, Nafam." The owner of the shop, a skinny man with slightly slanted eyes, dark skin, and a sweaty bald head, nodded at me and quickly wiped off the small table he was near. He pulled a stool back and smiled at me. "Thank you," I said as I sat at the stool. Karzin joined me.

"This makes you feel better?" he asked as he sat.

"That it does," I answered. I looked at Nafam. "Two orange sodas, if you please, and…what's the special today?"

"Of course," he said, then quickly yelled something in a language I did not know to the back. He turned back to us. "Today's special is Luurizi with chicken dumplings and vegetables."

"Sounds good. Two please," I said. Nafam went to the back while his daughter, a small girl of maybe thirteen, brought out our drinks.

"Damn," Karzin said. He had made a practice of trying to use human vocabulary more often. "These are some big drinks."

They were, at that. Nafam had come to recognize my tastes and knew that I always ordered the largest drink, a cup that numbered more than sixty ounces in size. I shrugged. "As for whatever the Puppet Master is, I don't have enough information to hypothesize."

"But, just for the fun of it, you think it's a creature that controls plants." He didn't phrase it as a question, but I knew he was asking.

"At least I think I do. It's the only thing that makes sense to me. What about you? What do you think?" I asked over a sip of my soda.

"This is good," he said as he took a drink of its own. "As for me, I just think it's a dumb beast or plant of some sort. It might have some intelligence, but it can't be as smart as us."

"Why not?" I asked. "The Xathi were."

"That's a different story," he said.

"Is it?"

"Yes," he said brusquely. "The Xathi were created to

adapt and that adaptability made them intelligent."

"Who says this isn't the same way?" I asked as I leaned back to leave room for Nafam to give us our bowls of ramen. "Oh, that smells good."

Karzin sniffed his own. "What is that smell?"

"It's either the Luurizi or the onion pepper he uses. It takes a little getting used to, but it tastes fantastic," I answered. "Try it." I dove into my ramen with zeal. Nafam was a genius at taking something as simple as broth, noodles, and meat and turning it into a fabulous meal that satisfied your hunger.

Karzin tried some. I watched his eyes go wide before he, too, dove into this meal.

There wasn't much conversation over the next twenty minutes as we finished our first bowls and then worked on our seconds.

When we were finished, Karzin leaned back in his stool, put his hands on his stomach, and moaned in pleasure. "You were right," he said. "Now I know why you eat here so often."

"I told you," I smiled. "Look, whatever the Puppet Master is, it's something that we'll deal with. We always do. However," I said quickly as Karzin started to speak. "I'm hoping Tella, Leena, and the others in the labs can give us more information when they're done. Then we'll decide on not only what to do, but also about what this is."

"You're right. You going back for more toxin?" he asked.

I nodded. "Yes, one more round, then going home."

"Ah, Nesta there with you?" he smiled.

I chuckled in embarrassment. "Yes, she is."

"To think, the two of us with our own humans to love. Did you ever think it possible?" he asked as he finished off his soda.

"Never," I admitted. "There was never a day after we crashed that I thought I would have feelings for anyone from here."

"And yet, now that we have them, I can't imagine having a day without them. Can you?" he asked.

I smiled as I paid the bill, leaving a nice tip. "Despite the fact that Nesta and I have only been 'together' for a few days, it seems like a natural fit, like a part of my own body."

"That's how I feel," he said. "Tell you what, give me the dart gun. I'll kill the next set of weeds. You go home and surprise your woman. Trust me, it'll be worth it."

"For the first time in a very long time, I believe that I will take the early time off. Thank you," I said as I handed over the rifle. Karzin headed off towards the lab, and I jogged home, plans for a surprise dinner running through my head as I went.

I wondered how Nesta would react to me greeting her at the door naked.

EPILOGUE: NESTA

It was the end of the week and there were only a couple dozen vines left. Anyone that had wanted to leave, had. The people that wanted to stay were still here, working on creating a way to start rebuilding...again.

I had been staying with Sylor for about five days, and I decided that it was time to take him to meet the people I had grown up with. I proposed the idea to him at breakfast and he agreed. I took him down and introduced him to Topan, Joe, and several of the others that were helping me make Sabre legitimate.

We spent the evening eating and talking. "No, no, don't tell him that story! No," I pleaded as Topan pulled Sylor closer. He was threatening to tell one of the more embarrassing stories of my life. Everyone was laughing about it and Sylor was smiling.

"It can't be that bad, can it?" he asked me.

"Oh, it's bad." I turned to Topan. "Don't tell him, please."

He winked and laughed.

"Don't do it, or I'm gonna tell about how you made a mistake with that woman," I threatened, my eyebrows going up and down rapidly.

"You wouldn't."

"In two seconds," I responded.

Sylor cut in. "Oh, now I have to hear both stories."

"No!" Topan and I said simultaneously. The entire table started laughing. Old man Sam actually started coughing as he laughed.

"I'll tell you," Joe said. "See, back when our lovely Nesta was six, oomph." He grunted as I hit him in the head with some mud from where a water spigot had recently been discharged.

"Don't you dare!" I shouted, laughing at the look on his face.

That started a small mud fight. It wasn't something we should have done as adults, but it was fun. I was aiming another ball of mud at Joe when a glob of mud hit me on the left cheek.

I looked over to see Sylor standing there, clean somehow, with a handful of mud and a smirk on his face. "Oh, you ass." I said as I threw my glob at him. He barely moved, but it was just enough to make me miss. He threw his handful at me and I hit the ground to avoid it.

The mud fight lasted a few more minutes before we finally called a stop to it. We were all laughing as we looked at one another. Topan had gotten the worst of it from how he looked. He was covered from head to toe in mud.

When one of the women, I think her name was Sophie or something, came over and took a bit of food off his plate and ate it, she cracked, "Mmm, you taste good." We all burst out laughing even more, Sylor most of all.

I was happy to see that he hadn't gotten away clean. He looked as if he had been hit by most of the mudslinging. His green skin mixed in well with what he was covered with.

I walked over. "You look good for a dirty guy," I joked. I cleaned a bit of dirt from his cheek and gave him a quick kiss.

I wrapped my arms around his neck, forcing him down to my level. I kissed him. He tasted sweet.

"This was fun," he whispered to me when we separated.

"Yeah, it was." I laid my head against his chest and held him close. We slowly began to move back and forth. After a moment, I heard a slight hum. It was coming from Sylor. It sounded like he was humming a song as we moved.

We were dancing. I sank even more into his arms and let his muscles carry me back and forth.

"Aww, you two are so cute," one of the older kids said as she walked by. "But, can you help out? Sheesh."

Sylor and I looked at one another and burst out into laughter. We kissed quickly, then pulled apart and got back to cleaning up.

A few hours later, everything and everyone was cleaned up. Topan found us as we were getting ready to leave. "You're not leaving, are you?"

"Well, it's getting to be a bit late," I said.

"Oh, come on. You finally introduce us to your boyfriend, he beats everyone in a food fight, and now you want to just take off?" Topan shook his head, grabbed me by the hand, and pulled me back to the party. "I don't think so. We got something we need to talk about."

"What about?" I asked as I pulled Sylor with me.

"Give me a second," Topan said. He led us to the center of the party where a stage had been hastily constructed. He pulled us onto the stage. "Can I have your attention?!" he called out to everyone.

The conversations died down quickly as everyone

turned their attention to us. Topan smiled as he looked at us.

"Now, I was never Nesta's biggest fan," he started with a gentle elbow in my shoulder. "But I think she's managed to prove all of us wrong. She's shown herself to be strong, intelligent, and a pretty good judge of character. I mean," he cleared his throat, "she chose Florina to be her second instead of me, so that has to tell you something."

"Yeah, that you suck as a leader," Joe shouted from a far corner. The crowd laughed and Topan nodded.

"Alright, alright. There's a minor point there," he said to another chorus of laughter and comments. "But! But at least she was smart enough to include me in her decision council, so, like I said, she's shown her intelligence."

"She felt sorry for you!" Sam shouted.

I stepped forward. "No, I didn't. He's got a good head on his shoulders, especially now that we're trying to be legit. He's a terrible criminal, but a pretty decent good guy." I put my hand on his shoulder and smiled at him. He nodded his thanks.

"But, that's not why I brought her on the stage tonight," Topan continued. "I brought her up here to thank her for helping us find our way." Whatever he tried to say next was drowned out by the cheers and applause. I felt a bit embarrassed by that adulation. I didn't deserve it.

"Now, I'm willing to bet that she's currently thinking that she doesn't deserve this," Topan said as the cheering died down. "But she would be wrong. She deserves all of this and so much more. As would her boyfriend, our new friend, Sylor!"

Everyone started cheering again. I looked up at Sylor and swore that I saw his cheeks darken. Was he blushing?

"This man has taken our rough and annoying Nesta and turned her into a fantastic person that we all like. Now, we've all admitted at one time or another that Nesta's a beautiful woman, but we all knew that there wasn't anyone down here that could handle her." That brought laughter and a few groans. "Okay, okay, awkward moment. Sorry," Topan apologized. "But, what I'm trying to say is this..." he turned to look at us. "Thank you, both of you. If you, Sylor, had not come into her life, she would not have matured and grown like she has. And you, Nesta, if you hadn't already been strong and stubborn as shit, we'd be falling apart instead of on a path to a better life."

The cheering overwhelmed the warren as Topan hugged the both of us.

"One last thing...Nesta is in charge of Sabre, and Sylor is hereby our newest member!"

The party went on for a few more hours before Sylor and I were finally able to sneak away. We made it back home, me leaning against his arm as my eyes got heavier and heavier.

"That was fun," Sylor said as he opened the door.

"It was," I said through a yawn.

"You're tired?" he asked.

I nodded, too tired to answer.

"Hmm. I thought we'd be able to 'celebrate' my inclusion into Sabre," he whispered in my ear as his hands started to travel up and down my body. My exhaustion was replaced with desire and I moved my head so our lips could meet.

I was home, and enjoying every second of it.

LETTER FROM ELIN

With every book I realized the world of Ankau is larger and more complicated than I originally dreamed!

Nesta and her underground weren't part of the original plan, but when I started wondering how we'd get past the Puppet Master's dome, I realized we had three options:

Over

Though

Or Under….

Now that the dome is gone, life will be easy for our valiant heroes, right?

snerk

You know me better than that.

The Puppet Master isn't defeated. But the crisis we'll be dealing with in *Iq'her* is closer to home.

Much, much closer.

Keep reading for a sneak peek!

XOXO,

Elin

I q'her

GENERAL ROUHR LET out a deep breath, sat back in his chair, and closed his eyes. "Estimates on how long our food supplies will last?"

"Unknown, sir. This could simply be a blight that is temporary or this could be the result of something far more sinister," I answered. "When Sylor killed the first set of vines, the numbers increased by nearly nineteen percent. In the subsequent weeks, with all of the vines making the dome now destroyed, the numbers had increased at an alarming rate of just over thirty-seven percent. More than a third of the plants on this continent, half of which were used for food, were either dying or dead."

"How quickly will that affect us?" Rouhr asked.

This would create a problem of nearly apocalyptic proportions before too long. During the near year that we'd been a part of the population, I'd noticed that many humans knew next to nothing of proper distribution, use, and storage of their perishable goods.

Of course, I was a bit biased and perhaps a bit spoiled. While living on the *Vengeance*, the food simulators were capable of taking the most basic of edible materials and could turn them into meals.

The simulators could take two tons of materials and feed sixty full grown Valorni three meals a day for an entire year. The simulators aboard the *Aurora* were even more efficient.

However, there was a slight problem.

"If I were to put a timeframe to it, I would say at current levels of consumption and loss, less than a year."

He let out a groan that sounded as though he had just been struck in the chest. "This is not something that I wanted to have to deal with," he said quietly. He never mumbled, but I wondered if he had said those words more for himself than for me. He looked up at me and rubbed his hands together. "So, what are your suggestions?"

"There are only two reasonable courses of action that we have, sir." I sighed. "For long term stability, both will require investigating if the Puppet Master is involved or not. We need to understand the connection between those vines and the rest of the planet's ecosystem."

"Tell me." He pursed his lips.

"Rationing, or finding ways to create new and more efficient simulators."

He cocked his head to the side. "Could we build enough simulators?"

I shook my head. "Even if we used every system from the *Aurora*, as well as every computer system in all of Nyheim and Duvest, we would not be able to create enough simulators to feed the entire population. We would be forced to eliminate nearly eleven percent of the population in order to feed them."

"And that's obviously a terrible plan." Rouhr sighed and shook his head. "What we need is to follow your original suggestion of rationing." He clicked a button on his office comm unit. "Tobias?"

Nothing.

Another click, and static answered.

"This thing hasn't worked properly all week," Rouhr muttered. "What does it take for a general to have working hardware?"

"Would you like me to take a look, sir?" I offered.

"No," he waved the offer away. "I know resources are still tight. Everyone is doing the best they can, there's just too much to do. I'll wait my turn."

He stabbed the button again.

"Sir?" finally came the response.

"Bring me the records of our city-wide food stores, if you please," Rouhr ordered.

"Will do, sir," Tobias' enthusiastic voice answered. I smiled at Tobias' optimistic nature. He had taken the tragedy that came with our arrival in stride.

"With the amount of food we have available, and I'm guessing based on the reports I read last week," Rouhr started. "We're going to have to share some of our food with the small settlements, and we still might not have enough."

"No, sir, we won't. At least not in the long run. If every major city donates food to help out the smaller settlements, we will still only make it through a year," I explained.

"I know." He sighed. "But, it will help the smaller settlements stay alive, and that is what we need to focus on. We need to find a way to save everyone, if possible."

"And if it's not possible, sir?"

"I'm not going to think about that for now," he answered. "Let's concentrate on right now and what we can do to fix all of this."

I nodded.

Tobias brought in the reports that Rouhr requested and we spent the next hour reviewing them with Vidia.

Finally, face tight with strain, Vidia looked up.

"There's really only one way to handle this, isn't there."

Rouhr wrapped his hand over hers and nodded. "Rationing. There's no choice."

Decision made, Vidia nodded sharply and rose. "I'll start telling people, and start contacting the other cities. This affects us all."

She left, Tobias in her wake, noting down the list items she'd already started making in her head.

"What about us, sir?"

He sighed. "You and the teams are going to need to be on patrol to make sure that first, the Puppet Master doesn't decide to stir up more trouble, and second, the people don't start to riot. And then we'll need to coordinate with the other settlements, arrange for distribution. You may need to set up guards for the food drops, just in case."

I nodded in understanding. It was the only reasonable way to proceed.

As soon as Vidia and Rouhr announced that we would need to start rationing, people would become upset. They would start demanding answers, and without any immediate answers to give, those upset people would then become angry.

Angry people weren't likely to listen to reason or take kindly to being asked for patience.

Rouhr reached for the desk comm. "Attention all strike teams. Effective immediately, we are instituting a mandatory rationing system. I repeat, effective immediately, we are instituting a mandatory rationing system. Meet immediately for details--"

Tobias rushed into the office, face white.

"Sir! The message... Your desk comm..."

Rouhr stopped. "What about it."

The human male swallowed, then again. "It didn't broadcast to just the strike teams channel."

Srell.

"Where. Did. It. Go?" Rouhr asked, every word falling like a stone into the silence.

"City wide emergency broadcast," Tobias whispered. "All over Nyheim."

"Srell." we said in unison.

"You better get out there," Rouhr commanded. "I'll contact the other teams to let them know immediately."

"Yes, sir," I said. I left his office and headed for the armory. I was going to need some protection.

Stasia

. . .

"CHUG! CHUG! CHUG!" Everyone screamed as they banged the bottom of their glasses against the counter. Roddik was standing on top of the counter, waving both arms in the air as he enticed the crowd.

Only when he was satisfied with the noise, the window panes already rattling in their frames, did he bring his beer up to his mouth. With the expertise of a man that was used to drinking far too much, he downed his pint glass in no more than two seconds.

The bar exploded with applause and congratulatory whistles, and the bartender went as far as handing Roddik a congratulatory free pitcher of beer. That wasn't a good idea, the way I saw it, but what I could do? I was more than tired of playing the responsible-older-sister part, and it wasn't like Roddik listened to anything I said anyway.

Ventil was one of those hole-in-the-wall bars that seemed to be impermeable to whatever happened in the real world, and even a giant alien invasion hadn't been enough for the owner to close its doors. No more than a watering hole, it still was my brother's favorite place in the whole city.

"C'mon, Stasia." He laughed, climbing down from the counter and draping one arm over my shoulder. "Cheer up, will ya? The vines are gone, the sun is finally shining again...have a drink and put a smile on your face."

"I'm having a drink." I held up my own beer. "And I am smiling." At that, I forced my lips to curl up and showed Roddik what must've looked like a snarl.

With a dismissive laugh, he pulled me closer to him.

"You should really lighten up, sis."

"Yeah, well, it's hard to lighten up after working double-shifts all week long," I said, but Roddik was no longer paying attention.

He, along with all the other men in the bar, had turned toward the various screens that lined the far wall of the room. The screens had been turned off just moments ago but, all of a sudden, they lit up with the city's emblem and the word STANDBY glowing under it.

"Attention, attention," a raspy deep voice boomed through the speakers mounted next to the screens. As for the image, it remained the same, the word STANDBY replaced with PUBLIC ANNOUNCEMENT. "Ladies and gentlemen of Nyhiem. We've just been told that effective immediately, we are instituting a mandatory rationing system. I repeat, effective immediately, we are instituting a mandatory rationing system."

When the announcement ended, there was no more raucous laughter inside Ventil. Instead, there was just a deep silence, one that was fraught with tension. What were the city officials thinking?

The whole city was still reeling from the vine incident, and now they mandated a rationing system out of the blue?

"This is fucking bullshit," Roddik spat, slamming his glass down on the counter. The foam tumbled over the rim, splattering on the greasy metal counter and making a few of the men pulls their elbows back. Roddik grit his teeth hard, a furious expression on his face, and pointed toward the dark screens. "Who the hell do these *people* think they are? Food rationing? We were going hungry just a week ago!"

While most of the men nodded their agreement, I merely sighed. Roddik had never really cared about pretty much anything, let alone politics or government. That changed after the Xathi invasion, and his political rants were a constant reminder of how much life had changed in Nyhiem.

"Damn right, Roddik!" A burly man shouted from the other end of the bar, wiping the beer foam from his beard with the back of his hand. "We're not their alien soldiers. We're not their subjects!"

"Damn right we're not!" Another voice said.

"They didn't even care to tell us why," another protested, and it didn't take long before the bar was housing a chorus of protests and complaints against the sudden rationing system.

The dome had cut all of Nyhiem supply lines for

long enough for most people in this bar had gotten to
know hunger intimately. Now that the vines had been
driven back, most people were looking forward to
resuming their normal lives. This so-called public
announcement really threw a wrench into those plans.

"Tell you what," Roddik started, climbing up on the
counter. This time, though, no one was chanting. The
mood was somber, and I could already see that it'd
become even more so in the days to come. "I've had it
with these fucking assholes!" Roddik cried out at the
top of his lungs, a vein throbbing on his forehead. The
crowd shouted out its agreement, and I simply sunk
deeper into my seat.

Why the hell was I wasting away my day off like
this?

I should just get up and go home but, somehow, I
found myself glued to my seat as I observed Roddik.
Even though people were eating up what he was saying,
I could tell he had already had one drink too many. I
couldn't drag him home, but if I left I was pretty sure
he'd get into trouble.

"These aliens come here, bringing war and death,
and we're supposed to accept their rule?" Roddik
continued, his voice reaching a feverish pitch.
"Seriously, does anyone really believe our lives are
better because of them? Just look at this city. Nyhiem
used to prosper before these creatures came here. Now

half the houses lie in ruins, and the people we love are going hungry! How much more of this are we supposed to take?"

I leaned back in my seat, slowly drinking my beer as I took in the scene. Most people were nodding furiously as Roddik spoke, and some of them were looking at him with more than just admiration. It was an unbelievable scene: Roddik had never been a leader of men, and I seriously doubted this was the right time for him to turn into one.

"But what the hell are we supposed to do?" Someone a few tables behind me grumbled. "You want to fight these things, boy?"

Roddik seemed stumped for a few seconds, and I could almost see the gears turning inside his head as he thought of an answer. "We don't need to fight," he finally said, his eyes burning with a kind of determination I wasn't used to seeing there. "I know that Nyhiem's no longer our home. The aliens have become our rulers, I've accepted that. Thing is, we don't have to stay here. They might want to rule the city, but they'll never rule us!"

"DAMN RIGHT!" A few people cried out. These drunken dumbasses looked more than ready to march down the city's main avenue and protest against their imaginary alien invasion.

They had a point.

There was no denying that life had become exponentially harder after these aliens arrived here, but who was to say they were the direct cause of all our grief?

I'd be willing to give them the benefit of the doubt, but too bad they were doing a poor job of explaining their point of view to the masses.

As unbelievable as it was, most people still had no idea where the Xathi had come from, or why the hell Nyhiem ended up encased in a vine dome.

I had no idea, and neither did anyone else.

Communication from high above had always been similar to the food rationing warning we just received: it was always a summary listing of what they wanted us to do, no real explanation given.

Sure, the government was entirely human. People like Vidia still held to their titles, but how much of their power did they really have with the aliens in town?

The way I saw it, the one in charge was now that alien general.

Not that any of it mattered.

Humans or aliens...they all kept the populace in the dark.

"Who's with me?" Roddik asked. "We can leave Nyhiem behind and start our own colony. No aliens, no war, no food rationing. Just us and the product of our own work."

That did it.

The moment Roddik was done, everyone in the room jumped to their feet and started clapping, some of them already chanting Roddik's name as if he was some goddamn war hero. I knew that when the morning came, and with it some brutal hangovers, a lot of these idiots would have already forgotten about this stupid rebellion.

I worried all the same: Roddik was planting some dangerous seeds in his buddies' heads.

"What do you say, Stasia?" Roddik finally turned to me, the only person in the room that hadn't gotten up from her seat. "Are you with us or what?"

I sighed.

Part of me just wanted to punch Roddik for putting me on the spotlight. The other half wondered about the possibilities. I wasn't that attached to Nyhiem, anyway, and moving out of this place could be the fresh start a lot of us needed…

Pushing my chair back, I rose to my feet.

"I'm with you, Roddik," I said, tipping my beer toward him. He smiled at me, beaming with pride, and that almost made it all worth it.

Almost.

IQ'HER

. . .

I LEANED BACK, attempting to stretch a terrible kink in my back, as the rest of Strike Team Two worked around me. We were in a warehouse on the east side of the city, several blocks away from our headquarters, attempting to organize and pack food crates that were intended for drop-offs in three of the nearby settlements.

Miraculously, Rouhr's announcement yesterday hadn't resulted in the terrible reactions that I had anticipated. Thus far, we had been lucky.

Not only were the people much less angry than I had anticipated, they had also been much more giving than I had given them credit for. Of course, with Tobias speaking with several of the pantry and restaurant owners, there were some people that already had an idea of what was happening, or at least had a rudimentary idea.

The restaurant owners and food pantries were donating food, as were several of the farmers. They had made the selfless decision to donate what they could in order to help others. I was surprised by that fact.

"You getting lazy on us, Iq'her?"

I looked over at Rokul and his smug little smile. Just because the behemoth was several inches taller and a few tons heavier than me, he thought it would be okay to make fun of me because I wasn't able to carry as much as him.

"Just stretching myself out, Rokul. Tella had too much fun with me last night," I joked. The rest of the team all groaned and jeered at my little rib at Rokul's expense.

He took it in stride, however. "Really? Hmph." He cracked his knuckles. "Tella would have broken you." He then tilted his head to the side. "Maybe that's why your back is messed up. You're too weak to handle my woman."

We cracked jokes at one another's expense for another ten or so minutes as we continued to load the crates when one of the *Vengeance* crew turned city guard came running in. "What is it, Hewl?" Karzin asked.

From a technical point of view, Skotan biology was fascinating. Hewl was one of the few Skotan's whose scales were a different color than his own skin, and his skin was paper-white. His scales, when brought out, were a deep purple in color. According to Skotan history, a very small population of Skotan, due to a genetic anomaly, had scales of a different color.

And as interesting as all of that was, it didn't make a bit of difference right now.

Hewl spent a moment catching his breath before

answering. "Sir, one of the delivery trucks is being attacked by a pack of humans."

We didn't wait. Karzin quickly ordered the other factory workers to finish packing the crates as we gathered our gear. We were out of the factory and on our way in less than a minute.

Hewl led us to where he had seen the attack on the delivery truck. We were on the move, at a near sprint, for nearly two minutes before we arrived.

What we found was a pack of fifteen or so men and a few women surrounding the truck. They were rocking it back and forth and I could see that they had already broken the truck...one of the axels was sitting on the ground at an awkward angle.

A few of the men were trying to open the doors.

Upon our approach, Karzin was yelling to gather their attention. "Stop! You people need to stop."

One of the men turned towards us and yelled an obscenity at us. He tapped a couple of his friends on the shoulder and pointed in our direction. The crowd began to turn towards while three of them continued to concentrate their efforts on opening the truck.

They didn't look destitute or starving.

I could have understood that.

They were just angry.

"What are you people doing?" Karzin asked.

"None of your fucking business, alien," one of the men said, pronouncing the last word like it was a curse.

Yup. Angry.

"Actually, it is. You're vandalizing and destroying city equipment, trying to steal food that doesn't belong to you," Karzin countered.

"This food *does* belong to us!" the same human yelled back at us. His dark skin and dark hair seemed to almost absorb the light as his deep bass echoed off the buildings surrounding us. "You bastards are trying to steal our food and we want it back."

"We're not stealing food," I shot back. "We're trying to make sure that other people, other humans," trying to emphasize that last word, "are fed. The plant life of your world is dying off and you're going to run out of food unless you start rationing. We're trying to help."

I wanted to let them know that we were all in this together, that we were *all* going to suffer badly, not just them. We were all in this together.

However, they didn't buy my explanation. "Shut the fuck up, you goddamn cyborg. You're lying to us. You just want to make sure that we're forced to obey you by keeping us too weak to fight back. That's why you're taking our food."

"No, we're not!" I fired back. "We don't want to control anyone. Food is running out. The plants and crops that we *all* use for food are dying off. We need to come together, ration our food, and share with one another. That's what we're trying to do here."

"We're telling you the truth," Takar said, stepping forward with his hands up to show that he meant no harm. "Walk away from the truck and we'll forget any of this even happened."

"Or what, Orange-boy? You'll try to arrest us?" a different man, small in stature and with a scarred face, spat. "You can't take us all on."

Rokul snorted. Karzin shot him a sharp look as Sylor whispered for him to be quiet. Things were not going to go well, I could feel it.

I quickly made sure that my safety was still on, then holstered my blaster. We certainly did not want to make this a deadly confrontation. I reached into my rear pack and pulled out my gloves.

I had spent a bit of time with Sylor after we had first arrived making these. They included a small electrical charge that only activated when struck. After numerous tests, we had finally managed to properly insulate them so I wouldn't get electrocuted when I used them.

I had a terrible feeling in the pit of my stomach that this was about to become violent.

"Please." I held up my gloved hands. "All we're trying to do is make sure that everyone, and I mean everyone, has food to eat. That's all we're trying to do."

"Then you guys stop eating our food and get the fuck off our planet," the little one snapped at us.

I dropped my head and I sighed. This wasn't going to work. "Believe me, my friend. If we could return to our home, we would."

"I ain't no friend of yours," he growled. Then he turned to his crowd of friends and I read his lips. "Get them."

"Reck," Rokul echoed my inner thoughts with actual sound. All of us, including Hewl, quickly moved our weapons away and defended ourselves.

We were outnumbered about three-to-one, and what they lacked in training, they made up for with numbers and hatred. Four of them came right for me.

I stepped aside and pushed one by me, letting Hewl —who was behind me—have that one. I ducked under a wild swing, answering with one of my own to the abdomen. The glove sent a small charge into the man, causing him to scream and jump back, holding his torso.

One of the women jumped in next, swinging a wooden club of some sort at me. I ducked and dodged once, twice, three times before I was able to get within her reach. Not wanting to hit her, but fearing that I had no other choice, I blocked her newest swing of the club and lightly brought my elbow into contact with her forehead.

She stumbled back, looked at me oddly, then snarled as she jumped at me. She was wild in her attacks and I finally had enough. Due to her wild attacks, I moved away from her. She wasn't in control of her club and the momentum carried her. She tripped and fell, the club managing to somehow hit her stomach.

She dropped to the ground, moaning loudly and struggling to breathe. I checked to see if she required assistance but was interrupted by a shout behind me.

I quickly turned around, blocked a blow from my latest attacker, and swung my leg around, sweeping his feet out from under him. Karzin quickly punched him in the head and pushed me to the side.

A large body flew by me and collided with Karzin, taking both of them to the ground. However, the human's momentum was too much and Karzin flipped him over, landed on top of him, and bounced the man's skull off the pavement.

I looked around and quickly jumped in to help Sylor, who was being attacked by two people at once. I rushed over, grabbed the smaller of the two by the shoulder and spun him around. My left hand connected with an electrical pop with his jaw. He spun around and fell, his already injured jaw striking the ground hard.

Sylor kicked his in the groin, then snapped his knee up into the man's head. That had apparently been enough for the humans as they began running away. Most of them anyway.

Three were unconscious and two were already being bound by the brothers.

"That was fun," Rokul smiled, a bit of blood dripping from his nose. He wiped it away and smiled again.

I shook my head. *Idiot.* This had been a disaster.

"Get these people secured," Karzin ordered the brothers. "The rest of us, let's get that truck taken care of."

I looked over at the truck. The front tires were flat, one of the rear axles was broken, and the windows were shattered.

The back doors had been broken open and at least one crate of food had been dumped on the ground.

This was bad.

An absolute disaster.

And it was clear, things were going to get worse.

GET IQ'HER NOW!

https://elinwynbooks.com/conquered-world-alien-romance/

PLEASE DON'T FORGET TO LEAVE A REVIEW!

Readers rely on your opinions, and your review can help others decide on what books they read. Make sure your opinion is heard and leave a review where you purchased this book!

Don't miss a new release! You can sign up for release alerts at both Amazon and Bookbub:

bookbub.com/authors/elin-wyn

amazon.com/author/elinwyn

For a free short story, opportunities for advance review copies, release news and the occasional cat picture, please join the newsletter!

https://elinwynbooks.com/newsletter-signup/

And don't forget the Facebook group, where I post sneak peeks of chapters and covers!

https://www.facebook.com/groups/ElinWyn/

DON'T MISS THE STAR BREED!

Given: Star Breed Book One

When a renegade thief and a genetically enhanced mercenary collide, space gets a whole lot hotter!

Thief Kara Shimsi has learned three lessons well - keep her head down, her fingers light, and her tithes to the syndicate paid on time.

But now a failed heist has earned her a death sentence - a one-way ticket to the toxic Waste outside the dome. Her only chance is a deal with the syndicate's most ruthless enforcer, a wolfish mountain of genetically-modified muscle named Davien.

The thought makes her body tingle with dread-or is it heat?

Mercenary Davien has one focus: do whatever is necessary to get the credits to get off this backwater mining colony and back into space. The last thing he wants is a smart-mouthed thief - even if she does have the clue he needs to hunt down whoever attacked the floating lab he and his created brothers called home.

Caring is a liability. Desire is a commodity. And love could get you killed.

https://elinwynbooks.com/star-breed/

ABOUT THE AUTHOR

I love old movies – *To Catch a Thief, Notorious, All About Eve* — and anything with Katherine Hepburn in it. Clever, elegant people doing clever, elegant things.

I'm a hopeless romantic.

And I love science fiction and the promise of space.

So it makes perfect sense to me to try to merge all of those loves into a new science fiction world, where dashing heroes and lovely ladies have adventures, get into trouble, and find their true love in the stars!

Made in the USA
Middletown, DE
27 January 2022

59023046R00166